D0106291

Coulrophobia
& Fata Morgana

KNIGHT MEMORIAL LIBRARY

Coulrophobia
& Fata Morgana

········· *Stories* ·········

Jacob M. Appel

Black
Lawrence
Press

3 1357 00246 8582

KMA
5/18

Black
Lawrence
Press

www.blacklawrence.com

Executive Editor: Diane Goettel
Cover and book design: Amy Freels

Copyright © Jacob M. Appel 2016
ISBN: 978-1-62557-953-9

All rights reserved. Except for brief quotations in critical articles or reviews, no part of
this book may be reproduced in any manner without prior written permission from the
publisher: editors@blacklawrencepress.com

Published 2016 by Black Lawrence Press.
Printed in the United States.

The stories in this volume previously appeared in the following periodicals:
"The Butcher's Music" in *West Branch*; "The Punishment" in *Arts & Letters*; "Pollen" in *The
Pinch*; "Boundaries" in *Passages North*; "Coulrophobia" in *Bellevue Literary Review*; "Saluting
the Magpie" in *Fourteen Hills*; "Fata Morgana" in *Folio*; "Hearth and Home" in *Confrontation*;
"Counting" in *Louisiana Literature*; and "Silent Theology" in *Apalachee Review*.

For Rosalie

Contents

· · · · · · · · · · · · · ·

The Butcher's Music

. . . .

Two days after she finds a packaged ham tucked in among the Passover brisket, the butcher receives a letter from her sister. Her sister is a professional musician who plays a Tecchler cello worth several times more than Rita's butcher shop and Rita's garden apartment and Rita's six-year-old Toyota combined. Her sister is also a rabid vegetarian. In this age of mobile phones and email, reflects Rita, when astronauts watch from outer space as their wives give birth, it is so damn like Tammy to send an aerogram handwritten on onionskin paper. She passes the letter around the cutting table, taking pleasure in the way the bloody glove prints of the stand-in meatmen are soiling her sister's delicate script.

"She's a big deal, your sister," says Langer. The octogenarian holds the letter to the light, squinting as though in search of a hidden watermark. "My old lady goes in for classical music and she lets me know what's what."

"I thought you and your sister was—how do you call it?— estranged," Finklebaum objects. Finklebaum is a squat, round-faced man with a hideous mole above his left eye. Rita suspects he doesn't wash his hands after using the toilet.

"We've had our ups and downs," she says. "Nothing to write home about."

She misses working alongside men she can trust. She'd hoped the letter might break the ice, but now she no longer wants to tell Finklebaum and Langer and Gonzales that she hasn't spoken to Tammy in three years, not since Papa's funeral. That all she knows of her sister—such as the cost of the cello—she has learned on the radio. From outside, she hears the muffled chants of her one-time employees: "*Union-Busting-Isn't-Kosher*" and "*Butchers-Aren't-Chopped-Liver.*" The seven idle meatmen take turns marching in a narrow rectangle between blue police sawhorses, decked out in their freshly-laundered whites, and every morning at opening, Marty Katz serves up a one-man rendition of "We Shall Overcome"—although it sounds more suited for *The Gong Show* than a labor action.

"Take *my* sister," says Finklebaum, splitting apart a lamb shank, "What a strikeout. Pardon my French, but I wouldn't piss on her if she caught fire."

"Vera has always been musical," adds Langer, still focused on his own wife. "She's a hot number out on that dance floor."

Gonzales flashes his gold front teeth and says nothing. The Guatemalan is mute from a boxing match—but he works miracles on the chuck steak and boils a mean cut of tongue.

"I'll be back in a few," says Rita as she tears off her apron. "Hold the fort."

She has sworn to herself that she won't bother Lance while he's working—he is technically her competitor, after all—but Tammy's note is too much. (She has also received another letter, registered mail, warning of an impending rabbinical inspection.) What Rita needs is a hug, a pep talk. Someone to remind her that life is worth the exertion. Yet even as she crosses the parking lot to the Gourmet's Paradise, ignoring the taunts of the strikers, she knows she will regret this moment of weakness. Lance Forand is a gifted cheeseman, sure, and a first-rate friend, but he's far from the right guy for Rita. He is somehow *too* easy-going, *too* comfortable in his own shoes. Not even remotely a tortured soul. Besides, he likes her because she is a big woman—they are both big-bodied people—and she can't help resenting him for not objecting to her weight. No matter how often she sleeps with him, he will *never* be the right guy for her.

The air inside the Gourmet's Paradise is damp and chilly and smells a bit like a public bus terminal. They have an entire room devoted solely to meats, a smoked-fish display as long as a tennis court, sixty vats of flavored olives. They even have a woman on-staff who specializes in artichokes. *Only* artichokes. How in hell's name is she supposed to compete with an operation that can afford to hire a professional artichoker? (Or are you supposed to say "arti-chokress"—is that feminist or just plain silly?) In any case, for all of their fancy-shmancy experts, the glistening new Gourmet's Paradise is nearly empty at ten o'clock on a Tuesday morning. The lone customer in the cheese alcove is an elderly woman sniffing the hunks of Parmesan while waiting for her bakery order. She has affixed the bakery number to her lapel like a brooch. Lance stands bent low over his wooden workspace, hand-grating a colossal, spindle-shaped cheese. When he sees Rita, he grins—revealing his crooked incisors.

"Try this," he says.

"Please, I don't—"

"It's called *Oscypek*. From the Tatra Mountains in Poland," says Lance, holding up a clear yellow slice between his thumb and fore-finger. "The first recipes date from the fifteenth century."

Rita lets him lower the morsel into her mouth. The flavor is sharp and salty. To Rita, it tastes like tears. "It's hard," she says.

"One hundred percent sheep's milk," explains Lance, glowing. "It's probably the oldest continuously-produced wood-smoked cheese in the world."

"I didn't come here to talk about cheese," says Rita. She does not want to cry while standing in front of the dairy counter, but she senses the tears rising behind her eyes. "Is there someplace we can talk?"

"I'm off in twenty minutes," says Lance. "What's wrong?"

What's wrong, she thinks, is that you can't see how upset I am. What's wrong is that I'm about to burst out sobbing onto the Cambert and you're working up to a goddamn lecture on cheddaring processes. "My sister's coming to visit," says Rita, waving the bloody letter like a battle flag. "Out of the blue. *I'll be giving a series of charity concerts in New York at the end of the month and I thought I might drive up to Westford.*' After nothing for three years. How am I supposed to respond to that?"

Lance reaches across the cheese counter, taking hold of Rita's hands. He turns her palms upward to expose the prominent veins in her wrists and kisses each of them. He calls these veins liferopes. "The way I see it, you've got two choices," he answers, matter-of-fact. "Either you see her or you don't."

"I can't not *see* her..."

"Then that's that," says Lance. "Anyway, is she really *so* bad?"

"There's the problem. She's not bad at all—at least in the way you mean. She bends over backwards not to do anything wrong. It's just that deep down she thinks she's better than me—and it drives me up the fucking wall."

"That's ridiculous. Better than you? You're the most amazing human being I know."

"I'm a butcher," says Rita.

"So? What's wrong with being a butcher?"

Everything, Rita wants to answer. But she is her Papa's daughter to the marrow. She loves butchering—the sense of craft, of accomplishment—except when Tammy is around. "There's a big difference," she says, "between being a pioneering woman cellist and a pioneering woman meat-cutter."

"Nothing sexier than a gal who cuts meat." Lance leans across the counter and kisses her on the lips, his massive body dislodging a pyramid of Appenzeller wedges. She relishes the tickle of his mustache. "Whoever said *music* tames the savage beast—or breast—or whatever—should have gotten hold of a cleaver," he says. "But what do I know, right? I'm just a glorified milkman."

Rita has an urge to tell him that she loves him—even though she doesn't.

. . . . .

Tammy arrives the following Saturday morning, driving a Jaguar convertible. The consortium of charities that is sponsoring her concerts cannot offer her an honorarium—that would alter their tax status in some arcane and inexplicable way—so they've made it up to her by renting out the most expensive car on the lot. The chassis is painted ash gray with black bumpers. The hubcaps gleam like circular saws and the silver trim, fashioned into lightning bolts, reminds Rita of bayonet blades. She would never want to drive a car like this. She'd be terrified of scratch marks, or pigeon droppings on the hood. That is another difference between her and Tammy. Tammy is confident.

Or at least Tammy *was* confident. The woman who steps out of the Jaguar is noticeably jittery, unable to keep her cigarette still in her hand. She sports reflective sunglasses and a floral-print batik kerchief—both of which would look stylish, even sophisticated, on a younger, thinner body. But the butcher's sister, never a spare woman, has put on considerable weight. Fifty pounds? Seventy-five pounds? Enough to build hoops of fat around her neck. These hoops jounce as her body quivers. Rita wonders if her sister has developed a drug habit or an eating disorder. Or both. The only thing unchanged about Tammy are her trademark woolen finger-warmers.

Rita is kneeling outside her apartment—the apartment they inherited jointly from their father, the apartment her sister technically still owns half of—tending a modest stand of crocuses and hyacinths. On her days off, she enjoys light gardening. (And it's good exercise too—maybe not *as* good as jogging or swimming—but it *is* exercise.)

"I wasn't sure I'd find you home," says Tammy.

"Well, you did."

Rita peels off her gardening gloves and tosses them into the wheelbarrow. She considers hugging her sister, but it doesn't happen. Instead, she stands arms akimbo and offers a non-committal expression—neither smile nor frown.

"I thought maybe you'd be out," says Tammy. "Or still at the shop. One of the Jewish holidays is coming up, isn't it?"

"But I'm not out," answers Rita. "I'm right here."

"I suppose you are."

Rita knows she should say something kind, but she is feeling defensive. She recognizes the psychological damage these visits can do. "You couldn't have chosen a more perfect day," she says. "Fresh as if issued to children on a beach." She recalls this last part from a book she was assigned in high school; she never finished the book—she rarely finished any books because she read too slowly—but she had fallen in love with that particular sentence.

"Let's drive someplace," says Tammy. "Someplace quiet—without too many people. I'm not up to being around people right now."

"Okay. You're the guest," agrees Rita. She wants to be accommodating—and, in truth, she's never ridden in a convertible before. "Let me just put my tools away—"

"Can't you leave them?" asks Tammy.

"Well, I guess." Rita looks up and down the block. "But only for a few minutes.... Anyway, I can't stay out too long."

"Hot date?"

Rita ignores this. She hadn't dated anyone for so long that now, frankly, admitting to a boyfriend embarrasses her. It seems almost unnatural *for her* to have a boyfriend. Even Lance didn't ask her out for months because he'd thought she was a lesbian. Or asexual. Also, she dreads telling Tammy that Lance sells cheese for a living.

The inside of the Jaguar is cluttered with fast food wrappers and scattered sheet music. It stinks of cigarette smoke. Tammy removes a wooden box of compact discs from the passenger seat and stashes it in the back beside her overnight bag. They drive in silence for nearly fifteen minutes before Rita thinks of what to say.

"When's your first concert?" she asks.

"Oh, that. Tonight, I guess."

"You *guess*? What are you playing?"

"Nothing you've ever heard of."

"Try me."

"Von Dittersdorf's Prelude in A Minor and Clementi's Milan Suite."

Rita gazes out the window at the burgeoning spring foliage. A rabbit darts through the low grass alongside the roadbed—and although the animal is not Kosher, Rita can easily imagine roping its feet and draining its blood through its neck. She has never heard of either Von Dittersdorf or Clementi.

"Something like Mozart," Tammy elaborates, "and something like Beethoven."

"Do you tell that to the audience? Now we're going to play something like Mozart and then we're going to play something like Beethoven."

"We don't need to," Tammy answers earnestly.

They loop around the reservoir and cross over the Van Buren Turnpike, then veer onto a rough dirt road. This is the state game preserve where Papa took them hiking as kids. In the mid-morning, the countryside is alive with catbirds and warblers. Kingfishers perch on low-hanging braches, diving periodically for prey. Hostile black-and-yellow signs warn against carrying firearms onto public land. Also against harvesting mussels without a license.

"The human brain is fascinating, isn't it?" chatters Tammy. "It's uncanny how you can go away for a long time and then come home and still remember the layout of the streets."

"You *have* been away a long time."

Tammy cuts the engine. Eyeliner is trickling down her cheeks. "I've done something stupid," she says. "Really stupid."

Rita knows that her own idea of stupid is different from Tammy's. But she imagines her sister is capable of forgetting her cello in a taxicab—like those spoiled nitwits one hears about on the news. Or maybe she has pinched rare recordings or musical manuscripts from a university library—in some sort of compulsive burst of kleptomania. That would just take the cake.

She follows her sister around the back of the vehicle, navigating an archipelago of mud puddles. Tammy pops the trunk. The encased cello—much to Rita's dismay—lies horizontally beside two paper shopping bags. From one of the beige bags comes the sound of whimpering.

"Jesus Christ," says Rita. It is a baby. A naked baby girl. What kind of lunatic locks a baby in the trunk of a car?

"I couldn't go through with it," rambles Tammy. "I did the one— and then I couldn't go through with it. You've got to help me."

Rita does not know what the woman is blubbering about. Then she peaks inside the other bag. The second baby, a boy, is the color of undercooked crab.

"I don't want to go to jail, Rita. You've got to help me. Please."

"Good God. What do you expect *me* to do?"

"Something, anything," pleads Tammy. "I don't know. Maybe you could cut them up and hide them."

Rita rocks the living child against her chest. She feels frantic—as though she might unravel—but the baby's presence is soothing. "Who the fuck do you think you are?" she says. "Good God! Just who the fuck do you think you are?!"

"I'm begging you," pleads Tammy.

"I should let you go to jail..."

"I know," says Tammy. "Believe me, I know."

"My boyfriend sells cheese, goddammit," says Rita—surprised by her own words. "You so much as blink the wrong way about it and I'll turn you in myself."

. . . . .

Tammy is for burying the dead baby immediately, somewhere in the dense woodland off the hiking trails, but Rita insists on thinking the matter through. She drives them back to her apartment complex and rifles her linen closet for an infant-sized blanket. Eventually, she gives up and swaddles the girl in an old cotton tablecloth. Then she sets a cup of hot tea in front of her sister. "When you're ready," she says. "You'll tell me all about it."

"There's not much to tell," says Tammy. She toys with her tea bag, coiling the string around her index finger. "You know how it is."

"Honestly, Tam, I *don't* know how it is."

"I don't either," answers Tammy. "It just happened. There was this intern at the philharmonic in Berlin—"

"Please don't tell me he was a college kid."

Tammy shakes her head. "Younger. Sixteen. Seventeen. I asked him at one point, but I've blocked it out..."

"*Sixteen?*"

"I never even told him…I was going to do something about it—you know—but I kept putting it off and putting it off—because the thought of the vacuum and all that, it just scared the shit out of me. I mean, what if they suck out something you need…? A liver or a kidney or Lord-knows-what….And then it was too late."

"So nobody knows about this? Nobody could tell?"

"I don't think so," says Tammy, smiling anemically. "I knew being a fatty would pay off one of these days."

"Some payoff."

"Anyway, I got the idea in my head that if I came here, you'd know what to do. That I could have the baby up in my old bedroom or something—and give it away….But I thought I'd have at least a couple of weeks. And then last night at the hotel…"

"Maybe it was the stress…"

"I didn't *set out* to do it. I was just so upset—overwrought, really….The pillow was right there…and then it was all over before I knew what happened…"

"Until the second one came."

Tammy nods. "I'm not a bad person….You have to believe me, Rita. I'd kill myself if I thought you didn't believe me."

"I don't know what to believe," says Rita. "The only thing I know for certain is that we need to buy formula for that child."

"It could have happened to anyone."

"I suppose so."

Tammy pushes the tea cup away. "Do you have to be like that?"

"Like what?"

"Judgmental."

"How can I not be judgmental, Tam? You've murdered a baby, another human being. *Murdered*."

"Why do you have to put it that way? You've got a freezer full of cold cuts and you don't hear me making accusations….I don't want to make excuses, but when you think about it, infants don't have any more cognitive ability that cattle . . ."

"I can't believe you're even thinking this."

"There are studies, Rita. I'm just saying."

"They don't put you in prison for killing cattle." Something about the word prison energizes Rita. She glances at her watch; it is nearly noon. "There's no point in arguing about this," she says. "What's done is done. Now you'd better get ready for that concert tonight."

"I'm not going. I'll tell them I'm sick."

Rita stands up. "Don't be foolish. Of course, you're going. You don't want to look suspicious." She can't believe she's talking this way, like someone out of a television crime drama. "You'll give your concert—and when you come back, we'll figure something out."

. . . . .

When Tammy departs—somewhat assuaged by a double slice of strawberry shortcake—Rita phones Lance to cancel their dinner plans. No, she isn't angry at him. No, she isn't trying to let him down easy. It's medical, she explains. A female thing. Why can't he *please* give her some basic privacy?

"Let's get married and have a baby," he says.

Lance says this every time they speak on the phone—he's being both playful and sincere—but this time Rita feels her skin go hot.

"I don't want to get married," she says.

"Ever?"

"Look, I've got to go."

She scoops the living baby into her arms, careful to keep her palm under its head, and she drives down to the Quick & Easy for diapers and formula—bracing its tiny body against her chest with one hand while steering with the other. Rita's mind is suddenly cluttered with additional responsibilities: finding a car seat, baby clothes, a pacifier. And there must be other necessities too, obvious ones, but easily forgotten over decades of adulthood.

Her errand proves anything but quick and easy. It turns out there are dozens of varieties of formula—containing whey proteins, containing casein proteins, with and without palm olein oil. Parent's Choice, Parent's Choice Plus. Super Similac. Carnation. Angled mirrors run above the highest shelves of the minimart—to prevent shoplifting—and she notices the salesclerk is watching her. He is a tall, elderly Sikh with a full hoary beard. Rita quickly selects the most expensive package of formula. It's like buying wine, she thinks. Wine for babies. She purchases enough diapers to survive nuclear winter—at least, a short one. When she checks out, the old man smiles approvingly at the infant.

"A beautiful child," he says.

He does not mention the tablecloth—which Rita is prepared to pass off as an ancient Jewish tradition.

"Thank you," she says.

"What is her name?"

Rita's mind goes blank. She has somehow forgotten that babies have names.

"Carnation," she blurts out.

"A beautiful name," says the clerk. "Very American."

Carnation. How ironic. While Rita rocks the infant to sleep— in a toaster-sized cradle she retrieves from the storeroom—she remembers the grammar-school Mother's Day pageants of her childhood. All the girls with living mothers wore red carnations. She and Tammy wore white ones. Maybe that is why they have no mothering instincts of their own. "Don't worry, Carnation," she whispers. "We'll find a mommy for you. A good mommy. I promise."

Rita feeds the baby her gourmet formula. After that, she kills time until dark. The entire afternoon is a blur; she picks up a magazine, but rereads the same sentence several dozen times. She takes a fitful nap on the sofa in the living room. The springs on the sofa are busted and keep poking her under the ribs. While she is dozing, Lance leaves a lengthy, apologetic message on her answering machine. Then another. Later, a mechanized voice named "Charlie the Computer" phones to offer her a "sensational deal" on a cruise vacation. Meanwhile, the infant dozes soundly, indifferent to the surrounding chaos, to her dead twin in the bottom drawer of the refrigerator.

The apartment feels frigid, draughty. When the last sliver of sunlight drops behind the tree line, Rita rummages through her closet again—this time for a shoe box. She finds one, but it is too small. Her second search produces a larger container left over from a pair of hiking boots. This fits perfectly. Rita lowers the dead baby into the makeshift coffin, touching its pallid little fingers, its postage stamp nose, its tiny uncircumcised penis. She removes one of the rusty free-weights from her father's old dumbbell—ten pounds— and places it gently on the infant's chest. Then, reluctantly, she begins wrapping up the package like a birthday present. Without thinking, she flips on the radio. Her sister is playing. Something like Beethoven. It is uncanny how normal everything seems.

Midnight arrives and Rita drives out to the public marina. She had fed the infant again and left her cooing in a makeshift crib fashioned from three bath towels and a plastic laundry basket. This is risky, admittedly irresponsible, but some things a child—even a newborn—should never see.

She takes a stroll on a long, abandoned pier. Many of the slats in the jetty are missing. When she returns home, her sister is waiting at the kitchen table.

Tammy is simultaneously chain-smoking and spooning choco-
late ice cream from the carton. "Did you . . .?"

"Everything is taken care of," says Rita.

Almost everything. At least ½ of everything.

The baby starts crying and they exchange uncertain looks.

. . . . .

They are not in agreement about Carnation. They cannot even
agree to call her Carnation. Tammy insists that it is her right to
name the child—it's *her* baby, after all, not Rita's—and that she
isn't ready for such a drastic step. Such a *commitment*. Rita doesn't
understand what's so drastic about giving the girl a name. If not
Carnation, then something else. Jennifer, Helga, Africa. Even Kar-
nation with a "K"! Obviously, not naming the baby isn't a viable
option. They argue in loud whispers, so as not to wake the subject
of controversy.

"I suppose we can let the new parents choose a name. They'll
probably change it anyway," concedes Rita. She has slipped into
her angora sweater and is sipping hot cocoa while her sister paces
the linoleum—although, at Tammy's weight, it might better be
described as shuffling. Has she *no* shame? Does she really refer to
herself as a fatty? Rita can hardly bear to look at her sister; it is like
peeking into a reflective glass, a warped and prophetic mirror. She
suddenly regrets the hot cocoa and pours the remainder of the
mug into the sink. Time to take control of her life. "I'll start calling
adoption agencies first thing on Monday," she says.

"Who says I'm putting her up for adoption?"

"What else is there?" demands Rita. "I can look after her for a
few days, but I'm not a parent, Tam. I just don't have that in me."

"I wouldn't expect that of you. Honestly—and don't take this
the wrong way—I wouldn't want you to keep her."

"What's that supposed to mean? Because I'm a butcher?"

"Jesus. Chill out. Because it would be a constant reminder that I wasn't raising her myself." Tammy opens the refrigerator and shuts it again—apparently dissatisfied with the contents. "Every time I came over here, it would be like salt in my wounds."

"Once every three years," snaps Rita.

Tammy stops pacing. She rests her stout arms on the back of a swivel chair. "Look, I'm sorry I disappeared."

"You should be."

"I can take the baby and leave right now, if you want. We can find a hotel room."

The suggestion sends a tremor of panic down Rita's spine. "You're not taking that girl out of this house."

"Are you threatening me? If I didn't know you better—if you weren't my sister—I'd think you were threatening me."

Rita isn't sure how to answer—but she realizes this is a turning point. Whatever she says to her sister now will last between them forever. But it is not only her sister that she's speaking to; it is also a murderess, the female heir to those Roman Emperors who used to impale babies on pikes. How the two can exist simultaneously in the same human form is beyond Rita's comprehension. "I'm sorry, Tam. But you don't really want to raise a baby, do you?"

Tammy sighs and rests her forehead in the cleft of her hand. "No, I don't want to raise a baby," she says. "But I don't want anyone else raising it either. God, how I wish it had never been born."

"Don't talk nonsense," says Rita.

"I wish I'd never been born," continues Tammy. "What a waste. All those years of training, all that conservatory, and in the end I'm just as fucked up as anybody else."

"There, there," soothes Rita. She rubs her sister's shoulder. It is the first time they have touched in many years.

.....

The next morning, Rita is late for work. The country has sprung forward to Daylight Saving Time, and she has forgotten to adjust her clocks. Since she does not trust her temporary employees with a key, they are waiting at the curbside—only a few yards away from Marty Katz and his proletarian jamboree. Gonzales and Finklebaum are seated on a wrought-iron bench, elbows braced on a wooden crate, arm-wrestling. Langer holds a box of jelly donuts under one arm; he is attempting to wipe a pink stain from his trousers with a damp handkerchief. The stand-ins pay little attention to the strikers—or to the other man waiting outside the shop. This last visitor stands erect, gaunt, spectacled, with a shock of blond hair and chiseled cheekbones. He might easily pass as an extra from a corporate promotion video of the 1950s. In point of fact, he is Rabbi Klemmel of the Orthodox Union. The *mashgiach!* To him, Sunday is a workday like any other.

"Rabbi Klemmel!" exclaims Rita. Instinctively, she reaches for his hand—and then remembers that he will not shake hands with a woman. "I'm so sorry," she apologizes. "I hope you haven't been out here all this time..."

"Only one hour," Rabbi Klemmel answers dryly.

Rabbi Klemmel makes Rita's palms sweat. This is his sixth inspection in three years, the minimum requirement to retain her *hechsher* certificate, and Klemmel has never found any cause for concern. Still, she is a woman, an increasingly secular woman— and to him, she must seem as alien as a pagan. He also has an unsettling way of raking his eyes slowly over everything, including her, as though he might be planning to harvest her organs. Rita fumbles with her keys at each of the three bolts. She wonders if Klemmel will be able to sense the blood on her hands.

"Baby killer!"

Rita's keys clatter to the pavement. She clutches the doorknob for support.

"Baby killer," Marty Katz shouts again. The rabbi holds his hand over his emaciated abdomen as though preparing for a bow; he appears queasy. "This woman takes the food out of my children's mouths. I got five kids—one, three, four, six, and nine—and this woman wants me to feed them off seven hundred dollars a week."

Several of the other men grumble their agreement. They call out ages and salaries—like bids at an auction.

"You're a rabbi," cries Marty. "Tell me, is this fair? Is this *just?*"

The *mashgiach* scratches his nose, silently examining the strikers.

"I had to lower wages," Rita explains sheepishly. "On account of the Gourmet Paradise."

"Indeed," says Rabbi Klemmel.

"It's all *treif,*" shouts one of the strikers. "She skimps on the brine."

"She serves hindquarters as sirloin!"

"She stocks catfish behind the counter!"

"And bacon!"

Rita retrieves her keys and manages to open the locks. The tiny bell jangles above the door—and, at last, they are inside. She flips on the fluorescent lights, which flicker twice and then glow. The rows of meat greet them. Constant, unchanged. Nothing in life is as reliable as a side of beef.

"Again, rabbi," she says, "I do apologize for all that."

"You'll understand," answers Rabbi Klemmel, "if I ask to look behind the counter."

. . . . .

Rabbi Klemmel rakes his eyes over the cutting boards. He rakes his eyes over the broiling ovens. He rakes his eyes over the displays of chopped meat and egg matzos and pareve packaged goods. He does not touch anything. One spidery hand never leaves his stomach; the other hardly ever stops scratching his nostrils. Every few minutes, he asks Rita a question about her hiring practices, her business hours, her method of sharpening blades. He holds forth at some length about why it is important to remain closed on the final two days of *Succoth*. Several curious customers—older women— gather around to listen. The entire inspection lasts four hours.

"I am satisfied," says Rabbit Klemmel. "Unfortunately, I fear that I will have to take into account that pork rind I found behind the counter."

Rita starts to protest—*damn Katz and his strikers!*—but the rabbi cuts her off.

"I'm joking with you, Ms. Gold," says Klemmel. "There is so much strife in our world. I think it is important to be able to enjoy a joke."

"Oh, a joke."

"Would you like another one?"

Rita is not certain whether he means a joke or an inspection. She nods anyway, at a complete loss for words.

"Why don't Jews eat lobster?"

It is just a joke, but still Rita feels pressure to answer. She comes up with nothing. "I give up, rabbi. Why *don't* Jews eat lobster?"

"Because it's not Kosher," says the rabbi.

Klemmel's eyes twinkle. Rita smiles back politely.

· · · · ·

She keeps the shop open late that night—on account of the upcoming Passover holiday—and it is eight o'clock when she finally retrieves the child from Mrs. Leary, the salty Irishwoman who occupies the neighboring apartment. The widow is a retired taxi driver, but she's been happy to earn some extra cash looking after the baby and oblivious enough to believe Rita when she tells her the tablecloth *is* a Jewish custom. *My niece*, the butcher says. *My sister's daughter.* But the words—though true—sound dishonest. Rita doesn't dare leave the infant home alone with its own mother. The second of Tammy's three concerts takes place that evening. Rita listens on NPR, placing the baby's delicate little head beside the radio. She has read that early exposure to Mozart can improve a child's intellect. She wonders if "something like Mozart" will do the trick. For dinner, Rita broils herself lamb chops. The meat is tender, juicy, a prime cut she's been looking forward to all week long. It is a relief not to have to eat under her sister's critical gaze.

After dinner, she changes the baby's diaper. Then she carries the tiny cradle into her bedroom and sets it under the window. "Moonbeams for Carnation," she says, soothingly. Or at least street lamps. Rita carefully examines the window sills for cold air currents and then cozies up under her own covers.

She dozes off, but she does not dream. She *never* dreams. When other people describe their own dreams, it is utterly foreign to her—as though explaining colors to a blind woman. Rita's sleep is more solid. More like death.

In the middle of the night, she awakens to a noise. Footsteps? Rita rolls over, hoping they will go away, but she senses a presence.

Her sister is standing in the middle of the room. Tammy is still wearing the woman's tuxedo from the concert, including a pink carnation in the lapel, but she has removed her shoes. She carries a large pillow in both hands.

"Tammy?"

"I was just checking on it," says Tammy.

Rita sits up in bed. She tries to make sense of what she sees. "I can't believe this," she gasps.

"I was just checking on it. On her. *Really.*"

"With a goddamn pillow?"

Tammy lowers the pillow to her side. "Fine, you caught me," she says. "But it's the easiest way. Can't you see that?"

"Are you out of your goddamn mind?"

"Don't get all high-and-mighty on me. You've already disposed of one body. I don't see how a second one makes a difference…"

"She's alive! That's the difference!"

"She's hardly alive. She can't remember anything or communicate meaningfully. It's not like killing a five year old…"

"You truly are sociopathic," says Rita—as much to herself as to Tammy.

"Please, Rita. It will be painless—and then it will all be over."

This is too much for the butcher. Her sister has been bending her backwards all weekend—and now the bough must finally snap.

"Get out," she says.

"Okay, I'm going. We'll talk it over tomorrow."

"Get out of my house," Rita shouts. "I'm done with this. As of right now. Take everything that's yours and get the hell out of here."

"Please—"

"I'll call the cops. I swear I will. They can lock us both up for all I care."

"Okay, I'm going," Tammy says. She walks quickly toward the baby, as though she will snatch it from the cradle.

"That's not yours."

Tammy pauses. She looks at Rita through the cold, dim light. "I hate you," she says. "You've got everything and I've got nothing—and now you're going to steal my own fucking baby … and I can't do a goddamn thing to stop you…"

"Out," says Rita, reaching for the telephone. "Out."

She waits in bed until she hears the front latch click shut. Then she walks over to the baby and watches her sleep.

· · · · ·

On Monday, Rita is the first customer through the door of the Gourmet's Paradise. She rolls the baby in front of her—in a buggy-carriage stroller that she's found folded in a crawl space beside her father's bowling ball. There is no way of knowing whether the pram was once hers, or Tammy's, or possibly belonged to a third child buried and forgotten before either of them was born. There is also no way—by merely looking at Rita and Carnation—that a passerby might guess their history. They are just another suburban mother and daughter on an early morning grocery run.

When Rita enters the cheese alcove, she finds Lance atop a stepladder, stocking imported yoghurt on the upper shelves. The wooden stairs creak under his weight. "I have something for you," he says.

"We need to talk," says Rita.

"In one second. First, you've got to try this."

Lance produces a small red package decorated with milkmaids and elves. "Norwegian *Geitost*," he says. "It's a sweet cheese. A lot like caramel."

"You're not listening to me," answers Rita. "I don't want you to buy me cheeses. What I want is for you to listen to me."

The cheeseman appears perplexed. "Can't I do both?" he asks.

Apparently not, thinks Rita. "Aren't you going to ask me something?"

Lance stands beside the stepladder, inspecting his rejected gift. "About the baby?" prods Rita.

"Oh, she's adorable," says Lance. "Whose is she?"

"She's *mine*," answers Rita.

Lance's smile fades rapidly. "You don't mean—?"

"She could be yours." The cheeseman bites his lower lip, and Rita realizes that he is counting back months. "What I mean is, we could raise her together if you wanted to."

"I don't understand," says Lance.

"You keep saying you want to get married and have a baby. Well, here's the baby. We're both yours for the asking."

She is prepared to explain the origins of the baby, or at least a sanitized version, but Lance's expression reveals that won't be necessary. He looks like a man who has lost a child, not gained one. Rita is not surprised by this; in fact, she is relieved.

"This is all overwhelming," he says. "A baby."

"Is that a yes or a no?"

"A baby," Lance says again. "I don't know what to tell you . . ."

"I'll let you think it over," says Rita.

Lance says something else—something she doesn't catch—but it is not important. She knows she will not hear from him for a while—and when she does, *if* she does, it will be on entirely different terms. That is probably for the best. She reaches out and squeezes his forearms tenderly, a goodbye squeeze. Then she turns the stroller around and steers it briskly through the electronic doors into the parking lot.

A warm breeze blows advertising circulars along the asphalt. Sea gulls orbit overhead. The dogwoods in the traffic island are just beginning to bloom.

Outside the butcher shop, Gonzales is smoking a cigarette. (He rides the public bus and is consistently early; Langer and Finklebaum, who carpool, are perennially late.) Marty Katz is doing his vocal exercises—coughing, gargling—in preparation for the morning's salvo of song. When he sees Rita, he spits.

"Enough, already," says Rita. "You've overcome."

"What's that?"

"You win. Nine hundred a month."

Marty motions for the other men to hush up. "You for real?"

"You beat me," says Rita. "Fair and square."

The Gourmet's Paradise may still put her out of business. But she cannot fight the competition and her own staff at once—especially if she's going to raise a baby. It also hasn't hurt Katz's cause that he has five young kids.

The shop foreman steps around the cordon. "What's the catch?"

"No catch. We'll sink or swim together."

Marty whistles. "We did it," he shouts—and then he begins to sing. Rita isn't sure whether he's imitating Pete Seeger or Bob Dylan or Barry Manilow. The other meatmen exchange high-fives and phone their wives on their cell phones.

"But you've got to stop singing," insists Rita. "You're driving away the customers." She shakes the hands of each of the butchers. "You know what? Take the day off," she orders. "*Paid* holiday. But come back tomorrow, ready to cut."

Rita promises her stand-ins two weeks' wages and hangs the "Closed" sign prominently on the door of the shop. Then she retreats into the cutting room with her new daughter and begins tenderizing a side of mutton. What she longs for now is a few hours alone, the momentary asylum of honest work. On the radio, they are replaying Tammy's first concert. Something like Mozart. Something like Beethoven. Rita listens for a few seconds and then shuts off the music. She continues pounding away with the tenderizer, softening the toughest flesh and humming along to the rhythm of the meat.

The Punishment

· ·

One sharp autumn night in 1944—before breasts, before boys—
Patzi Fierling perpetrated an avian holocaust in the gardens behind
the Episcopal cathedral. Her own building, the Samuel J. Tilden,
stood catty-corner at 110th Street. Its ground floor housed a psychiatrist's office. On Tuesday and Friday mornings, you heard the
patients screaming from the electroshock treatments. There was
also a candy shop, a dressmaker's, a chop suey joint. Young girls
dallied on the sidewalk, pitching bottlecaps, flaunting their skill at
clap-and-rhyme. Patzi's friends preferred the unchaperoned path-
ways behind the vicarage, where you might pluck feathers from
the rumps of the free-roaming peacocks or squat to urinate in the
beds of peppermint and watercress. Harmless fun. Until a bald,
fleshy official caught Patzi yanking at the tail of an agonized fowl.
The man—Patzi took him for the bishop, but now suspected he'd
been a groundskeeper—telephoned her parents. When Isadore
Fierling returned from his fur store, he heated a kettle of scalding
water and poured it slowly over his daughter's outstretched palms.
Next time, he warned. *The reformatory.*

The following evening, the Fierlings welcomed the *Sukkot*
holiday with a grand family supper. Isadore drank a lion's share
of the wine. He berated FDR for dumping Wallace, condemned

Truman as a greasy-palmed hack. Meanwhile, Patzi's mother and aunt rehashed the Bette Davis-Joan Crawford feud in the kitchen. Amidst the tide of in-laws from Brooklyn, from Fort Lee—the hat-tree full, enough coats on the beds for her cousins to form trampolines—Patzi had little trouble sliding the carving knife off the roast tray and concealing it in the folds of her skirt. When the platters of *babka* stood nearly depleted, she slinked down the service staircase. Outside, the streets were dark and quiet—as though blanketed with invisible snow. Squares of light limned the tar paper in the windows of the rectory. At first, passing under the columnar oaks that sheltered the garden gate, she had to feel her way blindly. Then shapes formed from the shadow: the marble statuary, the Japanese maples where the peafowl roosted. Patzi removed her skirt before climbing into the trees. This let her pin the birds' necks between her knees while she sliced. Several fowl awoke to the slaughter, crowing maniacally before she brought down her blade—but Patzi didn't even pause when their heads flopped loose in her lap. She'd decapitated all three males and a dozen hens before the bald groundskeeper grabbed her by the ankles.

. . . . .

Now she was seventy: an elderly woman retrieving her delinquent grandson from a suburban police station. She'd stayed trim, kept her hair long, moisturized—you wouldn't find her going to seed like Mary Travers or June Carter Cash—but even Patzi knew that no cosmetic ploy could pass her off as middle-aged. Occasionally, on the subway, at the gym, a flicker of recognition: "You used to be Patzi Fierling, didn't you?" Past tense. As historic as Woody Guthrie or John Philip Souza. But two generations had come of age since "Patzi and the Peacemakers" disbanded—since folk concerts had been relegated to the public libraries and Unitarian churches of small towns with geriatric hippie populations—and the only people who recognized her name these days were crossword aficionados. When the raw-skinned young cop at the counter had demanded her occupation for Daniel's paperwork, she'd said *retired.* That had been an hour earlier: Maybe they figured retirees had time to wait. Why hadn't she said vascular surgeon? Nuclear sub commander? Not that it mattered. She dreaded confronting her grandson. *And, sadly, she did have time to wait.*

The police station smelled of evaporated coffee, typewriter ribbon, unlaundered sweatclothes—an aroma institutional and vaguely Marxist—and the cops looked like extras from the Barney Miller show. Patzi found this reassuring. Otherwise, Elmcrest lacked redeeming features: a bedroom suburb of wide lawns and narrow minds. Its opulence even shamed the inhabitants. *We're from the Hudson Valley,* they claimed. *Westchester County.* How could Lauren have moved here? Hadn't both of Patzi's daughters been breast-fed, positively-reinforced, womb-exposed to Mozart? The Montessori method in school—supplemented vigorously, at home, by morsels of Piaget, Bruner, Vygotsky. Hadn't Patzi spoken frankly about masturbation and their father's suicide? Led them through the homeless city in Tompkins Square Park? Recognized the limits of progressive theory—that affection, like Tinkerbell's pixie dust, was the tonic to make children soar? Her reward: Amy in a cult, Lauren in prison. o-for-2. Patzi wrote the girls long letters, but she accepted defeat. What mattered now was getting things right with the boy.

She glanced at the wall clock. Not yet seven in the morning. Then she realized that she'd been waiting for two hours, not one— that nobody had bothered to adjust the hands to Daylight Saving Time. It was Sunday. The other occupant of the waiting area was a fidgety woman, half Patzi's age, whose husband phoned at fifteen-minute intervals. From eavesdropping, Patzi gleaned that their son had been Daniel's accomplice—but she felt no desire to connect with the young mother. They each had their own private hell. What good could come of sharing? Better to listen to the drone of the dehumidifier and to watch the ceiling fan churn the musty air. Patzi crossed to the window and rapped on the plastic. The raw-skinned cop behind the desk looked up, surprised.

"I want to see my grandson," she said.

"A couple more minutes," said the cop. "The chief is with him now."

It amazed Patzi that the chief was awake on a weekend morning. She'd been at the Chicago Convention in '68 and she still viewed all law enforcement officers as somewhat shiftless and latently sadistic. Unfair, she knew, but still—"I thought you said there'd be no charges if we paid for the damage."

Although this was Daniel's most serious brush with the criminal justice system, it wasn't his first. In June, his friend had been falsely accused of shoplifting at the Village Druggist. The manager had apologized. The boys came back the next day and shattered his windows with an aluminum baseball bat. From that episode, Patzi learned that the district attorney preferred restitution to criminal charges—at least where the children of local voters were concerned.

"Sometimes the chief likes to give juvies a talking to," explained the officer. "Scares them in the right direction."

To Patzi, this sounded neither wise nor legal. "You'd think a grown man would be above scaring children," she snapped.

"Grown woman," said the officer. "Chief Deluca."

Patzi had no opportunity to object further. On cue, the chief appeared in the cluttered office behind the plastic window. She was pretty, under forty. The antithesis of the female cops from Patzi's Greenwich Village neighborhood, the bulk of whom resembled Charles Laughton. Sexy police: another Elmcrest amenity. Following Chief Deluca, his hands clenched into fists, came Patzi's grandson. Daniel wore dark jeans and an oversized black sweat-shirt with a pointy hood. He'd stained his cheeks black—face paint? soot?—another indication that this overnight escapade had been premeditated. When the raw-skinned officer unlocked a side door, the boy shuffled out indifferently.

"He's all yours," said the chief.

Patzi nodded. The boy slouched against the wall of the antechamber, his face fatigued but defiant. His gaze met hers—eye to eye.

"Say, Mrs. Fierling," said the chief. "My father loves your music." She wanted an autograph, Patzi knew. It would cost nothing. All Patzi answered was: "I'm sure he's very proud of you." Then she pushed Daniel forward by the shoulder and they stepped into the October chill.

The police headquarters stood up the street from the municipal dump. Sundays were for depositing bags of raked leaves—and a long line of parents squeezed in this chore while their kids were at soccer practice. The exhaust fumes from their idling vehicles clouded the sidewalk.

"Did you bring my cleats and shin pads?" asked Daniel. "I can change in the car."

Amazing! The boy had destroyed an entire schoolroom—bashed in a skylight, hacked apart a piano, burned his teacher's family photos—all because the woman had read some girl's note aloud in class—and now he was worried about soccer.

"That skylight," said Patzi. "It cost $1200."

"We can afford that," said the boy. "You're rich."

She grabbed hold of his slender wrist. He tried to shake her off, but she squeezed into the bone. "Do you understand what you've done?" demanded Patzi. "They could have charged you with arson."

He looked puzzled. She realized he didn't even know what *arson* meant.

"You can't do that to other people's property," she said.

The boy shook his arm free and walked off toward the car. As little as Patzi knew about girls, she knew less about boys. She still remembered sitting with Lauren at the assisted reproduction clinic, under a poster depicting various high-tech procedures—in vitro fertilization, intracytoplasmic sperm injection—and lobbying her daughter to choose a female embryo. Especially, she'd argued, since there'd be no father. Maybe this male grandchild was her punishment.

Patzi unlocked the car doors and they sat side-by-side. She didn't have the emotional energy to start the engine.

"I'm not your mother," said Patzi. "I can't take this."

"What are you going to do? Punish me?"

The only punishments Patzi could think of were her father's. *Stand in the corner and hold this quarter to the wall with your nose. Buy a strawberry malted at the soda fountain, young lady, and mix in a full cup of castor oil.* And, of course, the hot water. Her daughter's house had a 190° spigot, so she wouldn't even have to heat it in a kettle.

Patzi sighed. "Yes," she said. "I *will* punish you."

"Like you punished Mom?" said the boy. "Mom said you let her do anything she wanted when she was little. That's why she ended up in jail."

Patzi didn't know precisely why Lauren had been sent to West Virginia in an orange jumpsuit—she chose not to know—but she understood her daughter's mortgage shell game had cost hundreds of retirees their homes. White-collar defendants don't get six years unless they've done something awful. "Your mother is in prison," said Patzi, "because she exercised extremely poor judgment."

The boy reached across the gear shift and turned on the ignition. He lowered the power windows. "You came to live here because you feel guilty."

Patzi sensed a twinge of arthritis in her knuckles. "I came here," she said, "because there was no other choice. Would you rather have changed schools and lived with me on Washington Square?"

Daniel didn't answer. The boy turned on the radio—loud, rhythmic noise—and she snapped it off. He folded his arms across his chest.

"Let's go home," he said.

"No," said Patzi, decisively. "We're not going home. We're going to Miss Wallberg's house so you can apologize for what you've done to her classroom."

· · · · ·

Patzi had encountered Miss Wallberg—for the first and only time—on Open School Night. That's how the woman had introduced herself, too: *Hello, I'm Miss Wallberg.* Not *Ellen Wallberg* or a straight-shooting *Ellen*. Patzi suspected this surname-only routine wasn't merely force-of-habit, but that it reflected more substantial insecurities. In her experience, elementary school teachers fit one of two molds. There were the "regressors": those women who, over the years, acquired the thought processes of nine year olds. Their intellects melted. They experienced wonder at the molting of butterflies, blushed at words like *gamecock* and *pussycat*. Amy—before she'd joined the cult—had been such a girl. The other variety of teachers, the "capos," ran their classrooms like POW camps: They thrived on controlling young children and brandished their power in acts of arbitrary resolve. Daniel's sixth-grade teacher clearly belonged to this latter set. A woman well-deserving of a thumbtack on her chair. In fact, shaking the teacher's limp and clammy hand, Patzi had asked maliciously: *Was that Miss Wallberg or Mrs. Wallberg?* The teacher, obviously nonplussed, clasped her hand to her blotchy throat and stammered: *Miss. For the moment.* But *now* that was beside the point. Ellen Wallberg's character would probably benefit from having her classroom periodically sacked and her personal effects pillaged, but this apology wasn't about Ellen Wallberg. It was about Daniel.

Okay, it wasn't *only* about Daniel. It was also about Patzi's letters. She wanted her daughters to see that she was doing right by the boy, that her third stab at "parenting" was canceling out her first two failures. She wrote both girls every morning—first Lauren, then Amy—detailing Daniel's Little League games, his dioramas of Ancient Egypt, his efforts to build a kite from bamboo shish-kebab sticks and a plastic garbage bag. Patzi wrote the letters on monogrammed cream stationery, laboring over each cotton page like a medieval scribe illuminating a parchment. It was impossible to hone all of her love into a few scraps of paper, but she tried. The girls didn't write back. In Amy's case, Patzi suspected her daughter never saw the letters. The Mission of Purity—that was the name of her cult—rejected the seven pillars of modernity: medicine, entertainment, education, banking, religion, science . . . and something else. They didn't even wear eye-glasses. Most likely, their "prophet"—Patzi had seen him on television: He wore a green visor like an accountant—used the letters as tinder. Patzi's other daughter, Lauren, phoned every Sunday; letters weren't her style. Daniel refused to write to his mother either. He hadn't written once in the nine months since the plea bargain. When Patzi asked him why, the boy said: *She doesn't write to me. She hasn't earned them yet.* It was the most telling idea the boy had ever expressed, a sure sign he possessed a moral compass, though Patzi obviously couldn't share it with his mother.

But a personal apology! What better way to redeem Daniel's mischief!

Patzi dialed information on her cellular phone—the phone she kept in the trunk of the Mercedes for emergencies. It turned out the boy's teacher lived one village over in Le Havre. No surprise. The former Huguenot settlement had risen to whaling prominence during the nineteenth century, but its tidy cape codders now housed professional starter couples and the region's public employees. You could buy an Elmcrest zip code for exurban prices. While Patzi scrawled down the address, Daniel wiped his cheeks with his sleeve.

"Stop that this instant," snapped Patzi. "I think Miss Wallberg should get a good look at what you've been up to." She eased the car into traffic. "Heaven help us," she added under her breath. "Just like a cat burglar."

The boy continued to swab his face. "I'm not apologizing," he said. "The bitch had it coming."

"Watch your language!"

"She took something that wasn't hers."

The raw-skinned cop had filled Patzi in on the details—her grandson had apparently been much more forthcoming when handcuffed in the back of a squad car. Patzi also knew the girl who'd written the intercepted note. She was a stunning child with delicate features, a fully-developed chest and a silver dolphin pinned through her navel. At twelve years old! In Patzi's day, they'd called that jailbait. (*No, fifteen had been jailbait. Twelve had been Raggedy Ann and hopscotch.*) In the way of childhood crushes, Daniel took pains not to mention the heartthrob's name.

"You shouldn't have been passing notes," said Patzi.

"Whatever. It's a free country."

Patzi had marched in Selma. She'd played Woodstock. She didn't need to argue about freedom. "There are different kinds of freedom," she said. "Miss Wallberg was exercising her freedom by reading your note."

The boy spun toward her, his face suddenly animated. "Part of freedom is a right to privacy," he said. "The right not to have your personal papers searched. Thomas Jefferson wrote that into the Declaration of Independence." He spoke rapidly, his nostrils flaring. He appeared genuinely aggrieved.

"Is that what they teach you? What ever happened to President Washington and the cherry tree?"

Daniel ignored her. "I'm not apologizing," he said. "I have nothing to apologize for."

"You can't take the law into your own hands," answered Patzi. She knew this wasn't exactly true—her entire professional life had been about civil disobedience, resisting injustice—but it *sounded* right. Convincing. The sort of hard-and-fast reasoning you should offer a sixth grader.

After that, they drove in silence. The homes grew smaller, older. American flags appeared with increasing frequency.

They pulled up in front of Miss Wallberg's duplex. It was the last structure at the end of a poorly-paved cul-de-sac. A jack-o'-lantern and several stalks of Indian corn ornamented the sloping concrete porch. The bulb above the front door was still lit, but light also poked around the curtains in the bay windows.

"We're here," Patzi announced.

"So?" answered Daniel.

He was resting his arms behind his neck. His legs were elevated, the soles of his sneakers braced against the glove compartment.

"Whenever you're ready," said Patzi, patiently, "you'll apologize to Miss Wallberg."

Daniel didn't budge. He filled his cheeks with air, then slapped them shut—producing a flatulent sound. He repeated the maneuver. Over and over. Eventually, reasoned Patzi, he'd grow tired. Or hungry—though the boy looked capable of digesting his own limbs before he'd bow to her pressure.

It was already nine o'clock. A man in a magenta bathrobe walked his schnauzer to the end of the cul-de-sac, then retreated to a house up the block. Across the street, a young father supervised his daughter's experiments with a plastic tricycle. Chipmunks capered along a stone ledge. Brown leaves rustled across brown grass. Patzi breathed deeply, willing her mind to relax.

The boy sat motionless, his eyes shut. Occasionally, he scratched himself—the only assurance that he wasn't sleeping. He appeared so fragile this way, so helpless. Then—suddenly, with no warning—he bolted upright.

"You want an apology," he shouted. "I'll show you an apology!"

He slammed the passenger door so hard that the entire vehicle trembled.

· · · · ·

Miss Wallberg answered the bell in a tight gray sweatsuit. The teacher wore a towel around her hair and burgundy toe polish, but no make-up. She looked as bleached and rumpled as an old bed sheet: ashen cheeks, frown lines, thin pallid lips. "Can I help you?" she asked Patzi—forcing a smile. Then she saw Daniel. Her face immediately reshaped itself into a look of mild displeasure.

"We met on Open School Night," said Patzi. "Patzi Fierling."

"Yes. I remember you."

The teacher still hadn't opened the door completely. She was standing two steps above Patzi, rendering them the same height.

"I thought we could speak with you a moment," said Patzi.

Miss Wallberg shook her head. "I can't allow this," she said. "It's nothing personal, but I don't keep office hours on weekends." She inched the door further closed. "You should call me on Monday to schedule an appointment."

"Wait," insisted Patzi. "Daniel wants to tell you something."

The groove deepened between the teacher's eyes. "I really can't—"

"It's a police matter," added Patzi. "It involves what happened to your classroom."

The teacher toyed nervously with her collar. Her look turned indecisive—Patzi could see her curiosity fighting her principles. *"What happened to my classroom?"*

"Can we please come in?" asked Patzi.

Miss Wallberg appeared shellshocked.

"We'll be gone in ten minutes," added Patzi.

Miss Wallberg nodded slowly. "Okay," she said. "Ten minutes."

She stepped back from the door, letting them into a long, dim corridor. The foyer contained a grandfather clock and an abstract sculpture on a pedestal. It was made from household products— Pepsi cans, Vaseline jars, Pampers. (To Patzi, it looked like a dog copulating with an elephant.) "This will really have to be ten minutes," the teacher added—too forcefully. "I'm expecting visitors."

They crossed through a small sitting room into a larger parlor. The room was sparsely furnished. Two black leather loveseats faced each other over a crescent-shaped glass table. On the table sat a bowl of small glass balls, also a book of Machu Picchu photographs and a copy of *New York Magazine*. The far end of the room opened onto a stark white kitchenette. Only a low slung cabinet under the window gave the space any personal touch. Here Miss Wallberg kept sepia photographs of deceased relatives, two Hummel figurines of school teachers, miniature porcelain teacups set on tiny saucers. The delicate curios filled both interior shelves of the case and every available inch of the surface—a scene straight out of *The Glass Menagerie*.

Patzi and Miss Wallberg sat on opposite loveseats. Daniel stood by the window, examining the Lilliputian glassware. "You've got an awful lot of cups," he said.

"Don't you touch those," answered his teacher. "They're from my travels."

Daniel shrugged. He tugged on the drawstrings of his hood.

"Okay," the teacher said. "What's this about?"

Patzi glared at Daniel. "My grandson has something to tell you."

The boy said nothing.

"Your grandmother says you have something to tell me," said Miss Wallberg.

Patzi held her breath—hoping desperately that the boy would come clean. The situation was far more awkward than she'd anticipated.

Daniel grinned. "Okay, I'll tell you," he said. "Last night, Tommy Pressman and me climbed up on the roof of the school and bashed in a skylight. Then we went to your classroom and we taught you a lesson."

The boy sounded exultant, not apologetic.

Miss Wallberg's mouth tightened. "I'm certain I don't know what you mean," she said.

"At first, we were just going to tear apart all those ugly posters you have on the walls—you know, the ones of Greece and Babylonia and all that. But then we had the idea of smashing up those trolleys you keep under the calendar. That's where Tommy's baseball bat came in handy. You should have seen it: It was like the world's worst train accident. Let me see... I guess next was the piano... or maybe the globe... yes, definitely. Did you know that globes are hollow inside—?"

"Daniel—!" interjected Patzi. She couldn't allow the boy's clinical account continue. "That doesn't sound like an apology."

"I'm telling her what happened," said Daniel. "Like you asked. I haven't even gotten to the part about setting her desk on fire."

Miss Wallberg was holding her hand in her mouth, biting into her index finger. She looked like a first-hand witness to the apocalypse.

"Enough of this, Daniel," demanded Patzi. "You're here to apologize."

"Of course," agreed the boy. His smile had grown broader, more confident—but he suddenly dropped his lips into a plaster frown. "I *am* sorry," he said. "You can't possibly understand how sorry I am, Miss Wallberg. Oh, no. This is an error that I'm going to regret for the rest of my life."

Outrageous! The boy was overemphasizing his words—not theatrically, but just enough to make a mockery of the exercise. Patzi contemplated dragging him out of the room by his ear, but she didn't.

"And on top of all that," he boy continued. "I'm sorry."

"Please," said Miss Wallberg—her voice hardly audible. To Patzi's surprise, silent tears were trickling down the woman's cheeks.

"Let's go," said Patzi, sharply. "That's good enough."

"But I haven't even told Miss Wallberg *why* I'm sorry," said Daniel. He glared at the unnerved teacher. "Do you know *why* I'm sorry?"

The teacher shook her head. "Please," she said again.

"I'm sorry," he said—practically shouted—"*that you didn't get to see me do it!*"

While the boy spoke, he cleared the top of the display case with his forearm. Photographs, figurines, porcelain cups—all shattered on the hardwood floor. "*You want more apologies!?*" he cried. Before Patzi could stop him, he kicked the case with full force and toppled it onto its side. Even this wasn't enough: He gave the overturned shelves a series of additional kicks, splintering wood. Then he stormed out—at first Patzi feared he might wreck the remainder of the house, but in seconds the front door thundered shut against its frame.

"Oh, God!" she apologized. "I had no idea—"

The teacher let out a hard breath. "Get out!" she said. "Now!"

"We'll pay for everything," continued Patzi. "Let me help you clean this up and we'll work things out."

"OUT!" shouted Miss Wallberg. "OUT!"

"I'll phone you," said Patzi.

"OOOOOOOOOOOOUUUUUUUUUUUUUUTTTTTTTT!"

"Okay," said Patzi. "I understand."

. . . . .

The night of the peafowl massacre, Patzi's father had picked her up from the Twenty-Seventh Precinct in her Uncle Wolf's Packard Roadster. He'd set an open suitcase on the passenger seat. It contained her clothing, also some bedding. *The reformatory, young lady,* Isadore declared in his heaviest Old Testament tone. *You've left us no alternative.* Apologies did her no good. To all of Patzi's tearful pleas—could she say goodbye to her mother? could she take along her stuffed rabbit, Flossie?—the inebriated furrier shook his head. *Your mother can't bear the sight of you right now,* he said. *Toys aren't allowed at the reformatory.* Through the Bronx, they drove. Across Westchester. Into the farmland of Connecticut. Patzi tried to memorize the route, so she could escape and sneak back, but the darkness proved unvarying and inscrutable. She struggled to offer alternative punishments: razor-strop lashings, icy showers, diets of lye soap. She sobbed until her eyes burned. Isadore didn't answer. And then, without warning, he veered into a potholed dirt lot. The surrounding hills were heavily wooded, but the silhouette of a mansard roof—possibly a barn, possibly a larger structure—poked over a nearby ridge. The headlights of the Roadster illuminated thick crabgrass, also two wooden signs reading PICK YOUR OWN MACINTOSH APPLES and PUMPKINS, 5¢ / lb. Isadore Fierling turned to his daughter and said: *You're lucky, young lady. They're all closed up for the night.* That was all he said—all he needed to say. It was nearly dawn when they arrived back in New York.

Patzi wanted to tell her grandson this story. She didn't want to frighten him or to let him know how lucky he was. No, not at all. What she wanted was for the boy to know how quickly life would spin by ... like the rolls of a player piano. She'd been driving through the darkness with her father—she could still picture the man's embroidered yarmulke, his droopy, wine-stained collar—and now she was driving with her own grandson. All of this was lost on Daniel, of course. The boy sat glaring at the dashboard. He wasn't even wearing a seatbelt. Silently, Patzi coasted her daughter's Mercedes into the driveway.

"You should have let me go to soccer practice," said Daniel.

Patzi ignored this. She opened the garage door and stepped into the house.

"It's not too late," Daniel said. "I'll change my sneakers fast."

Patzi walked up the staircase, bracing her weight on the banister. Her father had collapsed on the sidewalk at forty-six, spared the aches of old age. It was a trade-off: He'd also missed her music career, his granddaughters. What would the furrier have thought of a tap that spewed out water at one hundred ninety degrees?

The sink in Lauren's kitchen had been fashioned from burgundy ceramic. It was as large as a baby's crib, flanked by bronze faucets. Patzi rolled up her sleeves. She plugged in the stopper and filled the basin with scorching water. Steam rose off the surface in hypnotic waves.

The boy yanked at her elbow. "C'mon, Grandma," he said. "Okay, I'm sorry. She had it coming, but I'm sorry. Now please hurry up, so I don't miss practice."

"We'll go in a minute," said Patzi, gently. "First, slide that chair over here. I want to show you something my father taught me."

He stepped onto the chair. She circled behind him—catching him by surprise—and pushed his head forward into the water. Her entire hand felt on fire, but she kept the boy's face submerged. Daniel's cleats kicked her stomach, her thighs. She did not let go— not yet. With each passing second that her grandson's head flailed underwater, it grew easier to picture the young boy as an elderly man. She could already imagine the figure he would cut at seventy: wise, sincerely repentant, thoroughly above reproach.

Pollen

· · · · · · · · · ·

This story begins with one red rose, exquisite and ominous. Or maybe it begins fourteen years earlier, when my parents suffocated in an electrical fire up in Boston, and I was sent to Creve Coeur, Rhode Island, to live with my aunt and uncle. That's the tricky thing about family stories—you never know how far back you should go.

Let's start on the blustery October afternoon during my cousin's senior year of high school when Bill Anshaw appeared at the head of the porch steps, carrying a long paper funnel from his grandmother's florist shop. Charlotte was studying calculus when the door bell rang, sucking on a popsicle, her grubby white socks propped up on the kitchen table. Aunt Claire stood hunched over the sink, flabby arms elbow-deep in soapsuds. I was killing time. Skimming a magazine, pretending to be Jodie Foster. But I dashed to the foyer window, hoping Darren might be surprising me on the way home from one of his repair gigs, but knowing he wouldn't risk another run-in with my uncle. Instead, it was Bill: popular, bland, captain of our state championship water polo squad. Sweat plastered his short, dark hair to his temples. I'd let him kiss me once during eighth grade—in the airless cedar-paneled closet where Uncle Bernard stored pesticides and rusted fishing tackle—but that was all light years behind us.

I opened the front door. Twilight had already settled in—we'd fallen back to standard time that weekend; the wind chimes danced in the shadows.

"Heya, Becky," said Bill.

"You brought me flowers? How sweet!"

"Oh, no. They're for Charlotte," he said softly, self-consciously. Like he feared someone might mistake the messenger for the source. He tapped the wire basket on his bicycle, drawing my attention to the other bouquets. "And it's actually only *one* flower," he corrected himself as he handed me the meticulously-wrapped tube. "One red rose for Charlotte Dyle."

"Where's the card?"

"No card," said Bill. "It came in through FTD. Anonymous on request."

"Weird. Really weird."

"Yeah," he agreed. "I guess it *is* weird."

I shut the door and stood in the entryway, cradling the package. The blossom felt as weightless as the breath of a hummingbird. Aunt Claire emerged from the kitchen, drying her hands on her checkered apron. Charlotte followed. She wore beige corduroys and a ratty, shapeless sweater. It was hard to imagine anyone sending her a rose.

"Flowers?" asked Aunt Claire.

"They're for Charlotte."

"What a delight!" declared my aunt. "On your birthday, Charlotte Anne. How perfect!" She stood arms akimbo under the chandelier and watched appreciatively while I passed the flower to her daughter, as I though I were a maternity nurse presenting Charlotte with a newborn child. "Rebecca," she asked, "would you go get your grandmother's jade vase from the china cabinet?"

I didn't blame Aunt Claire for her excitement. Not once during my childhood can I ever remember her playing favorites between me and her own daughter. She loved us both too much for that. But a flower delivered to Charlotte was a special circumstance: I was, to be brutally honest, far prettier than my cousin.

Grandma Virginia's vase, long protected by a fine veneer of dust, left a circular scar on the cherrywood shelf. I had received my own share of roses through my first three years of high school, some pink, some red, from a multitude of different guys, and Aunt Claire had allowed me to fix them to my bedroom ceiling like stalactites, but she'd never carefully trimmed off the leaves and clipped the stems as she did with Charlotte's solitary blossom. While she worked, she sang, "People Will Say We're In Love."

"It's just a flower," said Charlotte.

"The first of many," answered Aunt Claire.

My aunt slid the rose into the tall vase and placed it smack in the middle of the kitchen table. Like a pioneer claiming a new continent.

. . . . .

The flower remained at the center of the table through dinner. Aunt Claire served birthday cake on paper plates and then we watched *Jeopardy!* on the black-and-white television set beside the refrigerator. Charlotte kept careful track of her score; on two prior occasions, she'd answered every question correctly. I enjoyed watching the contestants, trying to figure out what they were actually like in real life. During the commercial break leading up to the final round, Aunt Claire asked, "Didn't I say her ship would come in?"

I felt embarrassed for Charlotte. "We don't even know who it's from," she protested. "It's probably a mistake."

Uncle Bernard lit his pipe. He'd once been the rising star of Brown University's physics department, a pioneer in invisibility research, but then a team of Danish engineers had discredited his work as an optical illusion. In his forties, he'd taken to lecturing on the scientific underpinnings of Star Trek, and by the time I turned sixteen, my uncle's greatest worry was how early to plant his tomato seedlings.

He looked Charlotte over through a cloud of pale blue smoke and said, "It can't be very cost effective to send only one flower."

"Oh, Bernard," said my aunt. "Do you have to be like that?"

. . . . .

What inspired Darren and me to send that flower remains a mystery to this day, though I wonder about it often. A therapist might blame suppressed rage. Because Charlotte's parents had lived and mine had choked to death on thick black smoke. But it wasn't that—not that first time. Yet I'm confident it wasn't love either, or even kindness, though back then I would have sworn I was as selfless as Saint Francis. Maybe my impetus was nothing more than teenage curiosity, the desire to set the molecules of the universe spinning in unprecedented directions.

We'd gone out to North Jamestown, on Conanicut Island, where Darren had an appointment to fix the air conditioners at the Whaling Museum. Darren was smart—I told everyone who would listen that he was the smartest guy I'd ever dated—but school wasn't his thing. During his second round of sophomore composition, he sprayed his desk with Lysol and set it ablaze, bringing his days at Nathaniel Greene High School to a swift and decisive conclusion. Fourteen weeks later, he'd graduated from his HVAC crash course, and I was skipping classes to ride with him on his house calls. Darren got a kick out of teaching me about climate control while he drove, about the differences between CAV systems and VAV systems, but none of it sank in. Most of what I remember is pulling over at highway rest stops and making out in the dry grass beyond the picnic tables.

But the museum was hard to forget. They had a sixty-foot long sperm whale skeleton hanging from the ceiling in the lobby and the reconstructed forecastle of a Dutch schooner projecting from the roof. While Darren puzzled over why the ventilation system kept conking out, I explored the galleries of harpoons and scrimshaw engravings. What really got me were all those poor sailors, stuck for month after month on boats the size of our living room. Did they go crazy? Did they fall in love with each other? I had a theory that autumn that if you spent enough time alone with anyone, *anyone*, eventually you would fall in love. When Darren had finished tinkering with the museum's climate control, we explored the boardwalk overlooking Narragansett Bay.

The afternoon was warm, a final bout of Indian summer. I liked the refreshing scent of the sea air and the cries of the circling gulls. I liked the warmth of Darren's big hand under my cotton blouse, firm against my bare hip. I liked knowing that somewhere, elsewhere, my junior history class was inside learning about the Articles of Confederacy, or whatever, and that I wasn't a part of it. It felt like being on a honeymoon.

We bought a bag of salt water taffy at Mandy's Candies, and squeezed onto one of the wrought iron chairs opposite Ye Olde Flower Shoppe to gorge ourselves. Under the store's striped awning, buckets of cut flowers rose in colorful tiers: black-eyed susans, zinnias, snapdragons. Each time a customer passed through the doorway, a tiny brass bell jangled overhead. "You want to hear something fascinating," I said. "You can't tickle yourself. Try it if you don't believe me."

Darren folded one of the taffy wrappers into an origami goose and balanced it on my knee. "I think I should buy you some flowers," he said.

"Please, don't. You shouldn't have to buy me things to show how you feel."

I hadn't meant my words to sound so critical. I might as well have said: *I'm not for sale.* Darren's shoulders tensed and he gazed up the boardwalk toward the war memorial. The state and national flags hung limp above the antique cannons. I tried to kiss his neck, but he pulled his head away. "You read that in some bullshit magazine," he said. "About buying things..."

"Please, Darren—"

"I was trying to be nice," he said. "That was a lousy thing to say."

And that's when the idea came to me. A spark, from nothing.

"How does *this* sound?" I proposed. "Let's send flowers to Charlotte."

"Charlotte? I don't get it."

"Come on," I said, sliding off the chair. "Next week is her birthday. It'll be fun. She's much more appreciative than I am." I wrapped both my arms around the sleeve of Darren's leather jacket and tried to tug him with me.

"Jesus. What's gotten into you? You off your meds again?"

"You'll be doing a good deed," I insisted. "I think the reason Charlotte doesn't care about guys is because she's given up. That's why she needs a secret admirer—to motivate her to take better care of herself." I felt a surge of pride: What magazine columnist ever offered such good advice? "Besides, this will take her mind off college. She's totally stressed out about getting in."

"Me too," said Darren, grinning.

"Humor me, okay? I'll make it up to you."

I winked. Darren let me tug him off the bench.

"You're completely psycho," he said.

"I know," I answered. "I thought that's why you like me."

. . . . .

The flower did prompt some radical changes in Charlotte. She wore her hair down for school the next morning. It still had a stringy appearance, like unraveled orange yarn, but looked better than drawn up in a librarian's bun. Later in the week, I let her raid my closets, and she traded in her corduroys and sweater for a pair of acid-wash dungarees and a crimson halter top. She was thicker around the waist than I was, so she had to wear the jeans low—but this actually exposed a provocative sliver of skin at her hips. Charlotte resisted a complete makeover, unfortunately. She still wouldn't let me near her with an eyeliner pencil, or even lip gloss. But she'd made progress for a girl who, until two days before, had looked as sexless as a boiled sneaker.

My cousin had taken Grandma Virginia's vase to her bedroom and cleared a place for the shriveled rose on her nightstand. I passed her open door, one evening, on the way down to the kitchen. The room was still furnished with pink-trimmed white dressers left over from Charlotte's toddlerhood, but her walls were covered with posters of dead writers and philosophers. Mostly young women. Broad-faced, flat-chested, homely young women— although I know you're not supposed to say that—the sort of spinsters-turned-intellectuals who Charlotte would have been in an earlier century. My cousin lay on her stomach, writing in her journal. Her bare feet protruded off the end of the bed.

"You've got to hang that rose upside-down," I warned her. "Otherwise, the petals are going to flake off."

Charlotte slapped shut her journal. "Can't you knock?"

"Sheesh. I didn't know you were having such a private moment."

"Well, I was," she said, sitting up. "If you need to know, I was making a list of the guys who could have sent me the flower."

"Maybe it was a girl."

Charlotte ignored me. "You're going to say this is absolutely nuts, but I'm thinking it might have been Bill Anshaw himself. Why not? I mean, just because he delivered it doesn't mean he didn't send it."

"Anything is possible," I conceded. I stepped over a graveyard of library books—Elementary German, Smyth's Greek Grammar, languages they didn't even offer at Nat Greene—and retrieved the vase from the end table. "Now let's take this thing downstairs and tie off the stem."

"First, close your eyes," ordered Charlotte.

I squeezed my eyelids together and listened to the bedsprings wheezing as she stashed her journal between the wooden frame and the mattress. That's where I had discovered the notebook a few months earlier, while investigating her room. It contained nothing even remotely juicy.

"Okay, you can tie it off," said Charlotte. "But don't you dare ruin it."

"I know what I'm doing," I assured her. "I promise."

She put on her slippers—bug-eyed frogs—and followed me into the hallway.

"You know who else it could be?" asked Charlotte.

"A really hot girl."

"Dusty King," said Charlotte. "Stranger things have happened, you know."

Mr. King was Nat Greene's most popular English teacher, a former all-state baseball player. He'd led Columbia to an Ivy League championship and then returned to teach in Rhode Island. Every girl at the school had gone through a crush on him at one time or another—even I did, for a few weeks after Carl Carrano dumped me—but Mr. King already had an overweight wife in her late thirties and twin sons in kindergarten.

Charlotte followed me down the stairs and into the kitchen. Uncle Bernard had spread old newspapers across the Formica tabletop and was in the process of spray-painting birdfeeders. Several of the feeders were merely hollowed gourds, but one was a replica colonial farmhouse with a mansard roof. My uncle planned to color them all cadmium yellow, and the air stank like nail polish remover. He stopped spraying for a moment when we entered—as though to determine whether we were friend or foe, maybe even animal or vegetable—and then he returned to his efforts. Aunt Claire glanced up from the cutting board, where she'd been kneading ground beef for hamburgers. "Your hair looks gorgeous like that," she said. "Bernard, doesn't Charlotte's hair look nice?"

"Of course. Both of my girls are beautiful," said my uncle—as though recalling a script from memory. He shook the aerosol can beside his ear and kept on painting. "Did you girls ever figure out who that flower came from? Because you can probably call the shop that put in the original order."

"I want it to stay a mystery," said Charlotte. "Until my admirer chooses to reveal himself. He might have good reasons for preferring to stay anonymous."

"I see," said my uncle. He clearly didn't. I wasn't sure that I did either.

I set about preserving Charlotte's rose with the precision of a well-trained surgeon. First, I removed the flower from the vase and let it rest on the wooden counter, between the sink and the toaster. Next, I rummaged through the utility drawer for industrial-strength twine, a bag of colored pipe cleaners and an embroidery scissors. Then came the most challenging part: paring the bristles off a pipe cleaner and sliding the naked wire into the stalk of the flower. Finally, I tied off the stem—exactly seven inches below the head—and suspended the cord from the electric fan above the gas range. Not bad, I thought, for a girl with a sixty-one average in biology. I was an old pro at roses. My cousin looked on, not uttering a word, like a customer watching her butcher carve meat. But when I was done, instead of thanking me, she said: "He's not *that* much older than we are."

"Who?"

"You know who," she answered—but keeping her voice soft. Only then did I realize that she meant Dusty King. *Mr.* King.

"I think you're getting a bit carried away," I said.

Anger flashed across Charlotte's plain features. "What's that supposed to mean?"

"It *was* just a flower."

"Fuck you," snapped Charlotte.

"Language, Charlotte," objected my aunt.

My cousin sent one of the castered kitchen chairs rolling across the linoleum. "Why can't you just be happy that things are going my way for once," she shouted at me. "Why do you have to be so selfish? *You* get flowers all the time. But the minute a guy does something nice for me, you have to go ahead and ruin it." Charlotte broke into frantic sobs. "Fuck you, Becky. You're jealous."

I tried to squeeze her forearm reassuringly, but she slapped my hand away. Then she unhooked her flower from the oven fan, and carried it off to her bedroom.

"Poor dear," said my aunt. She frowned at me. "I'm disappointed in you, Rebecca."

"I didn't mean anything. Honestly."

Aunt Charlotte shook her head. "You can't *always* be the center of attention. It's about time you learned that. . . . Go apologize to your cousin."

"But I—"

"Go. *Now*," she said. "You're too good to be so petty."

. . . . .

I did apologize to Charlotte, and I let her apologize too, because she confessed that she'd overreacted, but I'm not sure either of us meant what we said. The next morning, instead of letting her drive me to school in her battle-scarred Plymouth Fury, the car that I was scheduled to inherit as soon as my cousin headed off to Harvard or Princeton, I took the public bus out to Darren's workplace. Serspinski and Gardullo, Steamfitters—S&G's—was a mom-and-pop operation that relied on a crew of local boys who weren't book-smart, or even particularly street savvy, but had mastered the intricacies of boilers and cooling systems. Most of these guys had military training. One of them, Davy Wendell, had even lost an eye while fitting hydraulic pipes for the navy. There was also a big black woman in her fifties, a grandmother of three. Gardullo, the late founder's nephew, didn't give a rat's ass who you were as long as you paid your union dues and knew what you were about with a wrench. Serspinski, who was also dead, had been a distant cousin of my uncle.

It was a sad, clammy morning. I sat on the damp curb, breathing on my fingers to keep them warm, waiting, daydreaming. (Grace Kelly had driven off a mountainside only a few months before, and every time I thought of her, my eyes misted up.) Across Meriwether Street—through the steel bars of the palisade fence that surrounded S&G's parking lot—I could see a trio of Portuguese teenagers unloading ceramic toilets from a mud-spattered truck. On a nearby bench, two crows picked at an abandoned box of pizza. Around eight forty-five, Darren's white van pulled in. One of his carpool buddies, a stocky guy named Oliver who'd been two years ahead of me at Nat Greene, jumped down from the passenger seat and crossed the wet asphalt toward S&G's office. Darren hoisted his toolbox out of the van before he approached me.

"What are you doing here?" he asked.

"I'm happy to see you too," I shot back.

Darren scanned the parking lot quickly and then rested his tool-kit on the fender of a late model Chrysler Imperial. "Gardullo's car," he explained.

I reached into his breast pocket and removed a soft pack of Newports. "How much cash you got on you?" I asked.

"Sixty, seventy bucks. Why? What's up?"

"We're taking a long drive," I explained. I lit a cigarette and dropped the pack into my purse. "We're going to send my cousin more flowers."

Charlotte wanted an admirer. Well, that's what she'd get.

"Shit, honey," said Darren. "I've got to work."

"Tell Gardullo something came up. Tell him you'll stay late."

I had a selfish streak in those days—back when I could fit into a size five dress. I still can't believe what I got away with.

"It doesn't work that way, Becky." He ran the toe of his boot around the edge of a water-filled pothole. "And I told my dad I'd help him with his gutters tonight."

"Help him tomorrow night," I insisted. "This is important."

"Wait here," said Darren. "I'll see if Gardullo will give me a long-haul gig."

I wandered over to the trash dumpster and carved my initials into the paint with a jagged stone. Ten minutes later, Darren came out of the office carrying a pink work order, and we drove out toward the east side of the bay. On the way, I explained what had happened between me and Charlotte.

"And you're sure you want to send her *more* flowers?"

"I don't like being screwed with," I answered. "I was just looking out for her and she screwed with me."

"Okay. You're the boss."

But I could sense he didn't approve.

We sped through the outskirts of Creve Coeur, where the ornate Victorian homes grew farther apart and increasingly dilapidated. Many displayed plywood boards in the windows; others had real estate signs on the lawns, and porches strewn with dead leaves, shrunken jack-o'-lanterns, clusters of mold-ridden Indian corn. We crossed over Route One—a brief oasis of chain stores and fast food joints—and followed a two-lane country road that wound its way between cauliflower farms and dairy pastures. Signs advertised "Pick Your Own Apples and Cranberries, 50 Yrds," but the orchards were padlocked for the winter. In Hogarth Corners, we saw the burnt-out husk of the local fire station—the one that had made the national news. On the radio, Aretha Franklin covered "Rose In Spanish Harlem." A steady rain started to fall, and Darren flipped on the wipers.

"Right there!" I shouted. He hit the breaks and they squealed.

The shop was named FLOWERS. Just FLOWERS.

"That's so Rhode Island," I said.

The air inside was an allergist's nightmare: warm, poorly ventilated, matted down with the scent of tropical pollens. Despite the shop's clear-cut name, most of its shelf space was devoted to potted plants: parlor palms, ivy baskets, dieffenbachia. Only a paltry selection of irises and tiger lilies stood in a pail behind a glass encasement. But we weren't actually choosing from these to send to Charlotte, of course.

Darren tried to strike up a conversation with a caged blue-and-gold macaw. I walked straight to the register and told the cashier what we wanted. He was a short bald senior citizen with an unkempt mustache—maybe somebody's peculiar great uncle.

"Anonymous?" he asked. "I don't think we can do that."

"It's for my twelve-year-old sister," I explained. "My father used to be a florist up in Boston and he'd send each of us a dozen roses for our birthdays—but then he left and we moved down here . . . and we want Charlotte to think he still cares." I tried to sound helpless, a trick I'd learned watching Aunt Claire. "Please. We'll pay extra . . ."

"You'll pay cost and not a dollar more. We florists have to look after our own. Like doctors and cops," said the florist. He opened his FTD pad. "Where in Boston did you say your old man worked?"

"The old part," I said. "Near where they had the tea party."

Darren paid the man forty-five dollars in cash. He would have chatted with the macaw again on the way out, but I didn't want the cashier to change his mind. On the sidewalk, Darren counted the money remaining in his wallet. "You're such a bullshit artist," he said.

"It worked, didn't it. But next time we need a different florist."

"Next time?"

"Let's go find a pull-off somewhere," I said, grinning. "I think I left something in the back seat."

"Jesus, Becky. I gotta work."

But instead, he parked the van along a muddy, densely wooded service road behind the Hogarth Municipal Dump.

. . . . .

Bill Anshaw appeared on the porch the following afternoon. He handed me a box large enough to bury a cat in. I was grateful for his timing: Uncle Bernard had just gotten off the phone with the assistant principal. We'd been ricocheting through a lecture on truancy and how Darren was a "toxic influence" on my future.

"Let me guess," I said to Bill. "Roses, and they're not for me."

"Sorry, Becky," he answered. "Looks like your cousin has a fan."

Charlotte came to the screen door behind me and practically yanked the package from my hands. Bill smiled at her. He was the sort of guy who could love a girl just because somebody else did. My cousin might easily have done worse. But she merely nodded at him indifferently and carried the roses into the kitchen.

I shrugged my shoulders at Bill and followed her.

"Saints alive!" exclaimed Aunt Claire. "We'll need a bigger vase."

"An even dozen," observed my uncle. "Now that's more sensible."

My aunt climbed onto a dining room chair and retrieved a porcelain jug from the top shelf of the china cabinet. She spent a good part of the next hour trimming and arranging the roses, singing to herself while she worked: "A Kiss is Just A Kiss." "The Yellow Rose of Texas." Fragments, refrains. When she was done, my aunt insisted on photographing both Charlotte and me holding the bouquet. "That's just glorious," she said, as the camera flashed. "The two most beautiful girls in Creve Coeur." I ducked out of the last few pictures so Charlotte could pose alone with her treasure.

"Do you know who you look like, Charlotte Anne?" asked my aunt.

Charlotte set the vase back down on the table. "Who?"

"Aunt Sandy, that's who. You're the spitting image of Rebecca's mother."

I could have clawed my aunt's eyes out for saying that. If I had any regrets about what I'd done to Charlotte, that was the end of them.

"What a wonder," continued my aunt. "You look so much like Sandy, honey, and I've always thought Rebecca takes after me. I suppose it's one of those mysteries of genetics—something like human cross-pollination."

Uncle Bernard and Charlotte exchanged amused looks; clearly, my aunt had said something scientifically doubtful. Then my cousin announced: "I've got a wacky idea. Why don't I write my Yale essay about this? About waiting for my admirer to reveal himself." Her theme, she explained, was to be the value of patience in a world obsessed with instant gratification.

When Aunt Claire drove Charlotte to Connecticut the following weekend for a second look at colleges—Yale, Wesleyan as a safety—I stole another peek inside her journal. It was better than I'd anticipated. She was thoroughly convinced that Dusty King was holding out for her until after graduation.

. . . . .

After that, Bill Anshaw appeared on our porch nearly every week. Sometimes he brought a full dozen roses, but on other occasions, he served up odd lots of three or nine, or once, approaching Christmas, seventeen. He'd clearly developed something of a crush on Charlotte himself—when I answered the door alone, all the joy drained from the poor boy's face—and at some point, I realized he was looking forward to the flower deliveries as much as my cousin was. What a strange soap opera I'd created! But Charlotte had her sights focused in a different direction. It didn't help Bill's chances any when three dozen red roses showed up on Valentine's Day with the note: "To my inspiration. Love, D." *That* delivery made Charlotte's admirer a subject of growing speculation at Nat Greene, and inspired two pages of fanciful musings about Dusty King in her journal, where she likened herself to the English writer George Eliot, luring her secret lover away from his wife. This elopement was to happen as soon as she started college in New Haven. But it was *so* like Charlotte not to mention that George Eliot was a woman, so I had to reread through her entry three times to figure out what she was talking about.

If I'd sent the second delivery of flowers out of anger, by the tenth bouquet I was operating entirely out of habit. Inertia. Because it was easier to keep the intrigue going, than to stop it. Or maybe I was addicted. There's no denying I felt a rush every time I helped Charlotte hang another set of flowers from her bedroom ceiling. The only drawback was that I had to get a part-time job to fund these floral binges. Darren grudgingly drove me to florists all over the state—I more than made it up to him with my tongue in the back seat of the van—but he wouldn't pay for Charlotte's roses any longer. I told him that this didn't make any sense: He would have been willing to spend the same amount of money each week on flowers *for me*. But he wouldn't budge. So eventually I got a job answering phones at S&G on Saturday afternoons. Uncle Bernard wasn't exactly thrilled, but he'd given up fighting me.

The problem with my aunt and uncle—from a parental point-of-view—was that they interpreted these random flower deliveries as evidence that their daughter was transmuting from a bookish duckling into a swan. Nearly three months passed before it crossed either of their minds that Charlotte's admirer might have a screw loose. The subject might not ever have come up at all, except that a swimming coach at a nearby high school had recently been suspended for stalking a neighbor's teenage daughter. The fallout dominated the local news for weeks. But when Uncle Bernard raised the possibility with my cousin that her mysterious pursuer might be a "middle-aged sex fiend"—he was never one to mince his words—she locked herself in his storeroom and threatened to drink what remained of the paint thinner. From that moment forward, nobody mentioned perverts and flowers in the same breath again.

Ironically, Charlotte and I grew far closer during these three months than we'd ever been before—and certainly than we have ever been since. She confessed to me that Bill Anshaw had asked her out to a movie. A Swedish film playing in Newport, because he'd thought she would enjoy that. "And I would have enjoyed it," said Charlotte. "Only not with him." She didn't say anything else about her crush on

Dusty King, but as March approached, she started calling home from school during the afternoon to see if a large envelope had arrived from Yale. Meanwhile, I took the SATs and did far better than anybody had expected. Then I got a tattoo of a shark on my ankle.

One evening, my cousin knocked on my door while I was sketching handbags. That was a phase I went through, where I wanted to be an accessories designer, before I returned to my interest in psychology.

"I just wanted to thank you," said Charlotte.

"Thank me for what?"

My stomach tightened. I was sure that she knew about the flowers.

"For not being jealous. I'd probably have clawed out your eyes."

· · · · ·

As far as I was concerned, I could have kept sending flowers indefinitely—maybe even after Charlotte went off to Connecticut. But as the spring advanced, Darren grew increasingly unenthusiastic. Gardullo took him river rafting in New Hampshire one weekend and promoted him to shift foreman. That meant more money, maybe even an opportunity to buy into the business someday. So Darren started talking about saving for a house, getting married, starting a family. *Making a life*. Every time he said the word family, I felt as though I was trapped in an elevator while it filled with scalding water. When I told him that *I already had a life*—that the last thing I wanted was to spend the next fifty years stranded in Creve Coeur, Rhode Island—he flipped out. "I can't believe that you'd rather torment your goddamn cousin than raise a family with me," he shouted. "That's just sick-o, you know that?"

The next afternoon—a Tuesday, during my Easter vacation—Darren hardly said one word on our drive out to Fall River, Massachusetts. We'd already exhausted nearly all the florists in metropolitan Providence, so he'd arranged with Gardullo to pick up some custom-fit parts across the state line. But when we pulled up in front of the "flower & garden center" that I'd found in the yellow pages, Darren refused to get out of the van.

"Do we have to fight about this now?" I pleaded. "This is an important week. She's going to hear from Yale any day now."

"I can't believe I've let this go on so long," Darren answered. "This is out of control, Becky. *You're* out of control—and you've really got to stop."

I was still furious that he wanted to marry me. "Or what?"

Darren pounded the horn without warning. A woman walking a schnauzer on the sidewalk looked over, surprised. "You've got to tell Charlotte what you've been doing," he added, raising the stakes. "What *we've* been doing. Or I'll tell Charlotte myself."

Something had hardened in his voice, and I suddenly recognized this was what he'd sound like as a husband. I took a long, deep breath.

"I'll make you a deal. Let me send one more bouquet and *then* I'll tell her."

Darren shrugged his shoulders.

I walked into the garden center and ordered four dozen roses. When I returned to the sidewalk, I was relieved to find Darren's van still waiting for me. But on the drive back to Rhode Island, when he tried to tell me about the boiler parts he'd picked up in Fall River—his way of bringing things back to normal—I gazed out the window and didn't respond. Finally, we drove up Banker's Hill and pulled onto East Clark Street. Charlotte sat on the porch step, reading, waiting for the mail.

"You'll tell her?" Darren asked.

"Yes, I'll tell her," I said, slamming the van door and shouting through the open window. "I'll tell her, you fucking control freak. But I never want to see you again."

That was the last time I ever did see him. He called twice, then gave up.

. . . . .

I crawled under my afghan and tried to blot out the world with my pillows. I must have been sleeping for several hours, maybe longer, when Charlotte charged into my room. She settled down on the edge of the bed and started bawling. At first, I feared that Darren must have told her about the flowers. Out of spite. But then I noticed the business-size envelope in her lap, and I felt instantly relieved. It was hard to feel too sorry for a girl just because she hadn't been accepted at Yale.

"You didn't get in, did you?" I asked. "I'm really sorry."

Charlotte shook her head. "I *did* get in. But then I drove to Mr. King's house, because I thought he was sending me the flowers..."

That was all she could say on the subject. She burst into tears again and kept repeating: "I want to die. I want to die."

"You're too good for him anyway," I said. I sounded just like my aunt. "It'll be okay. Honest."

I sat up in bed, drawing my knees to my chest. I'm not sure what inspired me to say what I said next, but I couldn't suppress the urge: "If I tell you something important, will you promise never to share it with another soul?"

"Not if you don't want me to," said Charlotte.

"It was Darren. *My* boyfriend sent you the flowers," I said. "He confessed everything this afternoon. He's your admirer."

I expected Charlotte to be shocked. But for a moment, she actually looked shattered—like a vessel fractured into shards. She started to speak several times, but didn't. Her first words were barely audible: "*Only* Darren?"

"Of course, it was only Darren," I said. Too fast. Too confident. "That's why I broke up with him."

My cousin's posture straightened. In that moment, I could already see her adjusting, recalibrating, contracting into the tight, distant adult she'd become. She stood up and walked toward the door. "Let's not mention this again," she said calmly. "I'm very grateful it was only Darren."

That was Charlotte's final judgment on the entire episode, her version of our family story: a silence so polite, but as piercing as thorns.

Boundaries

· · · · · · · · · · · · · · · · · ·

Artie Kimmel and I have worked the border together on Christmas Eve for each of the past eight years, because Artie's an agnostic Jew from Brooklyn, and because I haven't spoken to my sister since she shacked up with my ex-husband. Our long holiday night at the customs station has become something of an annual tradition between us, almost a religious ritual. I prepare honey-glazed ham with mashed potatoes and cranberry sauce, to be washed down with a mug of non-alcoholic eggnog, while Artie hooks his portable VCR into one of the security monitors. Not many drivers cross from Canada into Vermont on Christmas Eve—at least, not on Highway 19 between St. Gabriel and Danby Hollow—so we can usually enjoy Jimmy Stewart in *It's A Wonderful Life* without interruption. If anybody does pass through, it's likely to be an American tourist who's gotten lost on his way to the ski resort at Mount Sabine, or a pack of local teenagers, smashed as lords, taking advantage of the lower drinking age in Quebec. On a blustery, snow-ravaged night like tonight—when even the plows and salt-spreaders haven't made it this far into the countryside—we're not likely to encounter another human face before daybreak.

A frigid gust follows Artie into the office. He props his shovel against the filing cabinet, then spreads newspaper across the pine boards and stomps the snow from his fur-topped boots. Flakes cling to his beard, his eyebrows, the great barrel of his belly. "So much for Global Warming. If that's not another Little Ice Age out there, you could have fooled the long johns off me," he says, wiping sweat from his forehead with his orange wool cap. I get a kick out of how *"fooled the long johns off me"* sounds in Artie's heavy Jimmy Durante accent. "Maybe it's acute global *cooling*," he adds. "They say the Nineteenth Century Minimum came on without warning."

I don't know much about Little Ice Ages or Nineteenth Century Minimums, but I'm willing to trust Artie's opinion. He's not only a first-rate border agent, but he's also the most talented art-glass blower in Franklin County, as well as head docent at the local historical society, so he knows more about most things at thirty-four than I know about anything at forty-seven. If he told me we were actually slipping back into the nineteenth century itself, I'd probably believe him. The truth is that, except for the security cameras mounted on the eaves, our little colonial-style headquarters has hardly changed since my French-Canadian grandparents migrated south. Last year, Chief Crowley even found a sheet of unused three-cent stamps at the back of her supply closet.

"You've outdone yourself, Phoebe Laroque," says Artie, surveying the bowls of green beans and candied yams and chestnut stuffing crammed onto the folding bridge table. "This is truly a feast fit for royalty."

Artie offers this same praise every year—and every year his words flush warmth through my cheeks like a pitcher of red wine. "Merry Christmas, my dear heathen friend," I say, grinning, raising my mug of fake eggnog. "Bon appétit!"

"To the chef!" answers Artie. He taps his mug against mine—gently, like Eskimos nuzzling noses. "To the Julia Child of the North!"

He's not drunk, just enthusiastic. I wish I had one-tenth of his energy. Even when I was thirty-four and happily married to Neal—or when I *thought* I was happily married to Neal—I never loved life like Artie does. Not with that much gusto. I suppose if I'd been born beautiful—externally beautiful, like my sister, Valerie—I might have found such an intense joy in daily living. Or if I'd had children of my own. But things haven't turned out that way. Not even close.

Artie sloshes around his eggnog, gazing into the mug as though seeking liquid wisdom. "It's hard to believe it's been another year," he says.

I set down my own mug on the tabletop. "Does Julia Child have time for a smoke before we dig in?"

"I wish you wouldn't," answers Artie, "but I'll come with you."

He's been on my case for months to quit, ever since a former professor of his at Middlebury was diagnosed with emphysema. That afternoon he smoked his last Marlboro Light on the pedestrian promenade of the Ethan Allen Bridge, and tossed the half-empty pack into the gorge, hoping I might do the same. I couldn't, of course. But since Artie Kimmel is probably the only living soul who'd actually offer me a lung if I ever needed one, I can tolerate his well-intentioned badgering. He's even willing to brave the elements again, so I won't have to smoke alone.

The wind has picked up since nightfall—a fierce, penetrating wind as loud as a sawmill—and it's hard to distinguish the falling snow from the blowing snow. Up here, we call this sort of gale a "fishbowl cleaner," because the wind against your bare skin feels like the steel wool children use to scrub glass tanks. Drifts already rise waist-high beneath the drainpipes, and the visibility is so poor that the floodlights along the checkpoint don't even reach the nearest pines. Nobody will come through tonight. It will just be me and Artie—unless you count Henry Travers appearing as the Angel Clarence, showing Jimmy Stewart how worthwhile his life has been. And couldn't we all use a dose of that? I turn my back to the wind, hoping to light my cigarette—but it won't take. Then Artie crowds beside me, his arms raised, sheltering the flame from the storm. Soon enough, my lungs are filling gratefully with carcinogens.

"Thanks," I say. "For a heathen, you're a darn good friend."

This is a running joke between us, a Christmas Eve routine we've lifted from *Fiddler on the Roof*. It's funny because we're both as secular as Super Bowl Sunday, although Artie's a confirmed agnostic, while I like to hope there's something out there that's larger than ourselves—though Lord knows it's sometimes a challenge to believe that. What's remarkable is that Artie and I actually discuss these questions. After a decade married to Neal, I don't have a clue whether my ex-husband believed in God or an afterlife or the transmigration of souls. In any case, Artie usually responds with a quip like: "You're a good man for a gentile, Phoebe Laroque." But tonight, he remains silent and chips at the ice-glazed steps with the toe of his boot.

"You okay?" I ask.

"So there's something I've been wanting to tell you," says Artie. "I've come to a sort of realization."

"A good realization?" I ask. "Or a bad realization?"

"That depends," answers Artie. "I think I'm in love."

My first reaction is that he's in love *with me*. This is something we've never spoken about before—mutual intimacy of any sort. Maybe we're both too shy. Or maybe we've sensed that romance might disrupt the delicate harmony we've achieved. Also—to be quite honest—tubby, red-faced Artie Kimmel, as much as I savor his companionship, isn't exactly the knight in shining armor that a single woman fantasizes about. He must be a foot shorter than Neal.

I'm not sure what to say, so I take a deep drag on my cigarette.

"Here's what happened," says Artie. "I was out in the studio, trying to repair the pyrometer on the annealing kiln, when this college girl from SUNY Plattsburgh wanders behind the house, calling me by name. You're not going to believe this, Phoebe Laroque. She's driven all the way from upstate New York because she's seen photos of my cognac chalices and Zanfirico beads on the Internet—and she has a crush on me. A twenty-two-year-old pottery major from Schenectady!"

"That's wonderful," I say. "You must be flattered."

I feel like a previously-healthy patient who has just been diagnosed with terminal leprosy—that I won't really register anything else Artie Kimmel tells me. I'm careful to conceal my face behind my collar flaps.

"You're not going to believe this part. She actually calls her drive up here a *'pilgrimage'*—as though I'm J.D. Salinger or something," says Artie. "I should admit upfront that she's not the prettiest girl you've ever seen. Between the two of us—and please don't quote me on this—she looks a bit like a young Charles Laughton. But she really likes me. And let's face it: I'm not exactly Gary Cooper."

My entire scalp has gone numb. It seems an outrage that Artie Kimmel has fallen in love with someone else, that someone loves *him* and *no one* loves me.

"I took the girl to dinner at the Black Lion Inn," says Artie—naming the only upscale restaurant in Danby Hollow. "Her name is Dover. Like the sole."

"And you fell in love with her?"

My words sound less like an inquiry, more like an accusation.

Artie Kimmel says nothing. Instead, he stares at me peculiarly, as though he's strangled this love-struck coed and buried her corpse under his woodpile.

That's when the headlights appear. Two small, bright clouds poking their way through the darkness. Then the vehicle emerges from the squall, a rolling crate coated in frost and rime. It's one of those low-riding, foreign-made sedans you'd hire from a rental company, not even four-wheel drive. No chains either. Only lunacy or genuine desperation could inspire someone to attempt a border crossing on a night like this. The car—it's got Ontario plates— limps to a halt at the security barrier. Artie taps on the hoar-tinted window, and after a long, uncomfortable delay, the glass lowers in starts. Behind the wheel sits a dark-skinned young woman, her mouth shielded by a knit scarf, long black hair cascading over her shoulders. She slides a green passport out the half-opened window, revealing a tiny hand with fuchsia-lacquered nails. The white light against the white snow makes it difficult to see much of her face.

Artie flips through the passport and passes it to me. Our visitor is a twenty-eight-year-old citizen of Pakistan on a tourist visa.

"You chose some night to be traveling, Miss Khosa," says Artie.

Homeland Security has ordered us to make small-talk. It's part of the job. Terrorists, apparently, have poor cocktail party skills.

"*Mrs.* Khosa," she corrects him. "I am a very safe driver. Always very careful."

She sounds either annoyed or nervous—it is hard to tell.

"What is the purpose of your visit to the United States?" asks Artie.

"I am coming to look after my mother-in-law in the hospital," says Mrs. Khosa, her accent British and tightly-manicured—almost as though she's in pain. "She and my father-in-law have suffered an automobile accident on the way to Montreal."

Artie nods. He seems far less focused than usual—and he returns the woman's passport without asking any of the essential security or tariff questions. He hasn't even bothered to pan a flashlight across her backseat. Mrs. Khosa could be hauling kilos of uranium-235 insulated with cocaine bars, for all we know. But I suppose that's what love does to a person: You'll risk the welfare of the entire nation—maybe the welfare of the entire free world—to tell a coworker what happened on a dinner date.

"Okay, *Mrs.* Khosa," says Artie. "Welcome to the United States."

That should be that—but Artie, smitten as he is, is still unable to ignore the blizzard that has enveloped us. I sense he'd like this woman to vanish into the gloom, yet instead he asks, "Are you sure you'll be all right driving in this weather?"

A long pause follows. At first, I assume our visitor is thinking, weighing personal safety versus familial duty, but then I hear her struggling for breath. "I'm not feeling very well," she finally says, her voice markedly softer than before. "*I* need a hospital too."

Even my heartbreak—if that's what I'm feeling after Artie's revelation—doesn't prevent my border patrol instincts from kicking into gear: I flip on my own pocket flashlight and illuminate the woman's face. It's far worse than I could have imagined: Her skin is a sheaf of pustules, raised blisters like a million little bee stings. No curve of her face is spared—the eruption disfigures her eyelids and follows the coils of her ears. The scarf around her lower face has fallen loose, exposing sore-stippled lips.

I've only seen pustules like this once before. On the training video.

"Jesus-fucking-Christ," I say. "This can't be for real."

The driver answers me by collapsing face-forward onto the steering wheel. The vehicle responds with a short, urgent honk.

"Please tell me that isn't what I think it is," I say to Artie.

He removes the cigarette from my fingers and takes a deep drag.

"It isn't," he says, frowning. "Unless you think it's smallpox."

. . . . .

Chief Crowley is incommunicado, on a ten-day Mediterranean cruise with her daughters, so I phone district headquarters in Burlington. It crosses my mind that I may be interrupting somebody else's holiday tradition, maybe even a deep personal confession or an annual romantic tryst, but a case of smallpox isn't the sort of report you can postpone until the dayshift. When I tell the duty officer, Sergeant Steinhoff, why I'm calling, she first insists I'm mistaken and then falls momentarily mute—and in the background, I hear the courtroom scene from *Miracle on 34th Street*, Jerome Cowan asking Henry Antrim, "Do you or do you not believe this man to be Santa Claus?" Sergeant Steinhoff's supervisor, Captain Pritzger, instructs me not to let the victim exit her vehicle. We are all under official quarantine, he declares, until he can send up a HAZMAT squad. Obviously, with eighteen inches of snow on the ground, that won't be anytime soon. In the interirm, suggests Pritzger, our duty is to interrogate Mrs. Khosa about her most recent her personal contacts.

"He says not to bring her inside," I warn Artie, "and to question her thoroughly."

Artie looks up from where he has deposited our unconscious patient on Chief Crowley's black leather sofa. "That's what I love about working for Homeland Security," says my coworker, as he swabs the incapacitated woman's forehead with a damp dishtowel. "We're always one step ahead of the curve."

Mrs. Khosa is a slight, sharp-featured creature with thick eyelashes and a long, sinewy neck that makes her look a bit like a heron. Even without her pock marks, she could never have been mistaken for pretty—and this makes me feel for her. I can't help wondering if her husband remains in Pakistan, giving backrubs to her sister. Maybe her premature death is the good fortune he's been waiting for. That's when it first strikes me that *we* may very well die—*all three of us*. I don't remember what the precise survival rate is for smallpox—usually I do crossword puzzles during the training videos—but my instinct is that it's not very promising. And Homeland Security doesn't even issue us goddamn masks anymore, because Danby Hollow is considered a low-risk crossing. All I can do is rustle through the coat closet until I find a pair of musty bandannas, which will have to serve as makeshift air filters. When Artie and I wrap them over our mouths—his red, mine blue—we look like a pair of hyper-patriotic bank robbers.

"So what now?" I ask.

"I guess we should begin with the interrogation," says Artie. He turns to the limp body and asks, "So Mrs. Khosa—if that is your real name—is this your first attempt to smuggle smallpox across the border?"

I can't explain to you why this is funny. It probably isn't. But at that moment, it strikes me as absolutely hilarious.

"So you're taking the fifth, are you?" continues Artie, pacing the pine boards like Perry Mason. "It'll go easier for you if you tell us everything, Mrs. Khosa. Now think carefully before you answer this next question: Is all the smallpox you have with you *inside* your body, or do you have more of it concealed elsewhere?"

"We're going to die, aren't we?" I say. "We're really going to die."

Artie throws up his hands in mock-disgust. "I can't get anything out of her," he says, but his gallows humor shifts rapidly into outright anger. "She's a sick woman, you know. A human being! Did those bureaucratic nitwits in Burlington mention anything about sending an ambulance with their HAZMAT team?"

"I'm sure they'll send an ambulance," I say—though I'm not.

"I keep thinking I could put her in the pickup and drive down to St. Albans," says Artie, "but it's not like that's going to do her much good. Those morons would probably just quarantine the entire hospital until they could send up their lousy HAZMAT team. Or lock down the entire city." He crosses to Chief Crowley's desk and braces his chubby arms on the back of her swivel chair. In the next room, our Christmas dinner remains on the table, ham and beans and cranberry sauce all piled high and inert as though petrified by nuclear winter. Outside, snow continues to fall.

Artie disappears into the front office and returns with the ham platter. "I suppose we might as well eat," he says. "You have prepared a feast."

"At least we'll die on a full stomach," I say.

"Don't talk like that, Phoebe," he answers. "*Nobody* is going to die."

One glance at the cadaver-like figure on the sofa undermines any comfort that my coworker's words might offer. While Artie carries our meal into the chief's office, I rummage through our patient's handbag. It's possible to reconstruct her story from its paper trail: a computer print-out of her in-laws' itinerary in Canada, a Western Union telegram, the stub of her plane ticket from Karachi. There's also a wedding photograph and a second group portrait of the couple's four children. All girls. It appears that the parents of the husband were en route to visit another daughter when they drove off the Interstate just north of Duxville, and that Zahida Khosa has come to tend to their wellbeing, while her husband, a pediatric dentist, stays behind to earn a living. Where the other daughter is now, there's no way to discern. Other than documents and photographs, all the handbag contains is an emery board, a hairbrush, and an intricately-carved wooden giraffe. Probably a good luck charm. I find that I've judged Zahida Khosa by the contents of her purse—and that I like her immensely. "It's going to be all right, Zahida," I say, taking her clammy hand in my dry one. "We'll get you back to your daughters. Somehow." She groans in reply, squeezing my fingers—a flicker of promise in a sea of delirium.

Artie and I consume our meal one course at a time, emptying
the bowls and trays in the order he has retrieved them. Ham. Next
string beans. Then potatoes. It's as though we're taking part in a
carefully-choreographed ceremony, although for the life of me, I
couldn't begin to explain our behavior. We're halfway though the
candied yams when Zahida Khosa awakes with a violent jolt. "I
must go," she declares, but in a distant, groggy voice. "My mother-
in-law is waiting for me at the hospital. She'll be frightened." Something in the way she says this lets me know that her father-in-law
has been killed in the accident. My own father shot himself while
I was in high school—the shock still feels fresh to me, the moment
that cleaves my life into halves—so I can almost forgive the father-
less Mr. Khosa for his philandering. *Almost.*

"You're very sick, Mrs. Khosa," says Artie. "Please lie down until
the doctors arrive. If you need anything, we'll help you."

Zahida makes no effort to get up. I offer her another cool com-
press, but she shakes her head defiantly. Instead, she retrieves the
brush from the end table and attempts to untangle her hair. Then
she makes the most remarkable request: "Tell me a story," she says.
"Please, Mani. Tell me a bedtime story."

"The fever is making her hallucinate," says Artie, still chewing
on a mouthful of yams. He feels her forehead with the back of his
hand. "Yeah. She's burning up."

"Poor darling," I say. "I wish we could do something."

I remember when my own sister had pneumonia as a second
grader, and I skipped field hockey practice to read to her from
Mary Poppins Comes Back. That was the summer after we lost Papa
and I was terrified that Valerie would die too. But she didn't. She
recovered well enough to earn her nursing degree and to steal my
husband out from under my nose—so well, in fact, that she now
has the gall to deny that she wrecked my marriage. That's what

makes it impossible for me to forgive her: not that she was screw-ing Neal behind my back, but that she doesn't even possess the decency to admit it. She wants me to suffer the additional humili-ation of pretending that their relationship was entirely proper until the divorce papers were inked, while we both understand that this is an outright lie. And although my name is not Mani, and I know nothing of Zahida Khosa's childhood, I sit down beside her and start to tell her a bedtime story.

"I was also a married woman once, just like you," I say, "to the first man who ever asked me on a date . . ."

I tell the delirious woman everything: how one night after the break up, I'd gone to hurl myself off the Ethan Allen Bridge, but had merely vomited over the railing instead. How Val and I visited Mama's hospice room in shifts, so I wouldn't have to lay my eyes on her. How my sister will phone at ten o'clock, as she's done every Christmas Eve for the past eight years, and how Artie will inform her I'm taking a nap. I even reveal to our visitor how much I loved Neal—which I admit I did, maybe too intensely—how his warm body made the cold world tolerable. I realize I'm not saying any of this for Zahida Khosa's sake, but for Artie's. I want him to hear what he's missing out on—to feel guilty for preferring Dover Sole.

When I've said all I can bear to say, I tuck my patient's damp hair behind her discolored ears and kiss her gently on the forehead. She is out cold. I can sense the tears stinging at the corners of my eyes, but I don't wipe them away.

Artie, who has listened attentively during my story, rises abruptly and walks to the window. "Still snowing," he says, matter-off-fact.

"Why don't you see if you can get a weather forecast on the TV?"

The office television belongs to Chief Crowley. It's a black-and-white Zenith that her daughters left behind when they went away to college. Artie adjusts the rabbit ears and flips though the channels. We can just make out the sound through the static.

It's a CBS News special report: "Smallpox in Vermont."

The network runs an archive photo of our stationhouse on a warm summer afternoon and then cuts to footage of the ongoing blizzard. It's the same story on the other major networks: talking heads discussing incubation periods, lethality indices, patterns of dissemination. A man in a bowtie insists this "incident" has all the makings of a full-scale terrorist attack, while a retired lieutenant colonial argues that human error at a Russian research facility is probably to blame. Every few minutes, the news anchor reminds viewers that nothing has been confirmed—that it may be twenty-four hours before the authorities can reach our distant border outpost, that even the military helicopters can't get through the whiteout. Homeland Security has lost touch with us, he adds; our telephone lines have gone down. I reach for Chief Crowley's desk phone and check for a dial tone, but it appears the news networks have called this one correctly. My sister will not be phoning at ten.

Artie flips off the TV. "Wow," he says. "So much for a quiet holiday."

I feel like I'm on one of those television reality shows—suffering in isolation as the entire planet watches. I wonder what my sister is thinking. Whether she feels guilty.

"I never finished my story," Artie says. "About that girl from New York."

I cut him off before he can unburden himself. I've already done enough listening duty for one evening. If I'm going to be exterminated in a bio-terror attack—or whatever this is—I don't owe anybody a painful emotional crisis before my painful physical death.

"You'll tell me later," I say. "After we've seen the movie."

Then I pop the tape into the VCR and watch Jimmy Stewart rescue Bedford Falls from Lionel Barrymore's gluttonous bank. I want desperately to escape into the film's predictability, but it's more-or-less impossible to distract myself from reality with Zahida Khosa whimpering and thrashing on the nearby sofa. I wonder if this poor woman has ever seen *It's A Wonderful Life*. I wonder if she'd enjoy it.

. . . . .

"Maybe you should call her," suggests Artie. "She *is* your sister."

I'm attempting to coax Zahida into taking a sip of ice water, but everything I pour against her slack lips dribbles down the corners of her mouth. "You heard the man," I say testily. "The phone lines are down."

"I didn't mean tonight," Artie explains. "I just meant, in general."

I sense that my "bedtime story" has genuinely gotten under Artie Kimmel's flesh—that, if nothing else, he feels guilty for preferring Dover Sole to me. But I'm frustrated that he won't even take sides in my clash with Valerie—that he wants to remain neutral, to appoint himself goddamn arbitrator. How the hell would he like it if Miss Dover Sole shacked up with *his* brother? If ten years of *his* pent-up qualms and suspicions proved true. More than true—so true they almost seem false. If every time *he* looked back on *his* Thanksgiving dinners and family celebrations, *he* had to rethink what was going on during his spouse's long absences from the table. That's what I want to demand of Artie Kimmel: to ask him who the fuck he thinks he is to referee *my* family conflict. But instead I take a deep drag on my dying cigarette nub and say, "I'd rather drive down there tonight and cough some of my smallpox in her direction." Not that I'd really do anything that evil. As much as I can't forgive Valerie, she *is* indeed my sister.

I offer Artie a Virginia Slim and place a fresh one between my own lips. Under ordinary circumstances, Chief Crowley would have my head for lighting up in her office—but these are far from ordinary circumstances. The rational side of me wonders if there aren't still precautions to be taken, if we shouldn't stay as far away from Zahida Khosa as possible. But somehow, her very presence makes our fate seem irreversibly determined. Artie must sense the same thing, because he lights my cigarette and then his own.

Artie lets our patient's arm fall limp onto the cushions. "It's a thready pulse, but it *is* a pulse," he says. "At least my college first-aid course is paying off."

"Is thready *bad*?" I ask.

"It's all relative," he answers. "The bottom line is that she needs a doctor."

Artie folds Zahida's arms across her chest. They rise gently with her shallow breaths. "I didn't speak to my brother once for nearly six years," he says. "When I moved up here after Middlebury. But then 9-11 came along and I decided there was too much hatred in the world already, so I called him."

"What did you fight about?"

"Nothing. Everything," says Artie. "Mort was nineteen years older than I am. He paid my way through school—and he expected I'd come back to Brooklyn and help him run the family business. High-end Prostheses. Limbs, jaws."

At first, I think Artie's joking. About the limbs and jaws. But he's not.

The entire room is suddenly still. Deathly still. Even the wind has died down to a low, hostile moan in the distance. I watch Artie staring at our bedridden companion, his chin resting on his fleshy mitten of a hand. I realize that if Artie Kimmel loved me and not Dover Sole, I probably would end up phoning Valerie. Life works that way, one contingency feeding into another. I'm about to say something to this effect to my coworker, just to test the waters, when the phone rings. In my imagination, the console appears to jump off the chief's desk, like the rotary devices in Warner Brothers' cartoons, triumphantly announcing the restoration of service.

"I'm very glad I called Mort. He had an MI the following summer," says Artie, as he picks up the telephone receiver. Then his tone hardens and he identifies himself to the caller. "Officer Arthur Kimmel. Border Patrol."

Artie faces the wall while he listens, saying little—an indication that the caller far outranks Captain Pritzger and the Keystone Cops of Burlington. I sense he does not want to be interrupted. When he hangs up the phone, he appears relieved.

"Good news," he says to me. "They should be here in under an hour. And they're sending an army medical unit."

That means we're *not* going to die. I don't think. Already, I'm worrying about the cigarette smoke in Chief Crowley's office, and what will become of the leftover stuffing, and whether, if I *am* quarantined, this will count as sick leave.

"Do you hear that, Mrs. Khosa?" asks Artie. "You're going to make it."

Zahida's vacant eyes stare up at him. She hasn't made it.

· · · · ·

We've decided not to phone back the National Guard generals to let them know that Zahida Khosa has died. Somehow, we both sense that it is better to let them discover this on their own—to give our new friend's lifeless body a few more moments of tranquility before the prodding and jabbing begins. Soon enough, she will no longer be Zahida Khosa at all. Just the woman who died of smallpox. And Artie and I will either be the other two people who died of smallpox, or the pair who were quarantined, but got lucky. A thought flashes across my mind that they will place Artie and me on an island *together*, just the two of us, like lepers or victims of a mutiny. "At least Zahida's not going to be locked away somewhere like Typhoid Mary," I say. "How long do you think they'll keep us in isolation—assuming we don't get sick."

"Probably a few weeks to be safe," says Artie. "And for what it's worth, Typhoid Mary—Mary Mallon—didn't even carry typhoid. It was a mistaken diagnosis."

I slide a cylindrical throw-pillow under Zahida's neck, letting her beautiful dark hair stream free. The breadth of Artie's knowledge never ceases to impress me. "Two weeks isn't very long," I say—which is true. I had imagined we'd be locked away together for months. "You can handle that long away from Dover."

Artie shakes his head. "I sent her home," he says.

"Back to Plattsburgh?"

"Plattsburgh. Schenectady. Wherever," says Artie. His face has turned a deep crimson—blotched with purple—and his voice surges with a fiery intensity. "That's what I've been trying to tell you, Phoebe Laroque. I was out at the Black Lion Inn with this devoted girl who seemed genuinely in love with me . . . and I wasn't the slightest bit interested." Artie pauses nervously, as though deciding whether to keep going. I'm not sure where he's headed, so I smile encouragingly. "That's the big realization I came to," he continues. "I wasn't in love with her because I'm in love *with you*."

I don't have a chance to respond. Instead, as quickly as he's confessed his love, Artie begins enumerating his shortcomings. "I know I'm not the wealthiest man in the world—forget the world, I'm not even one of the wealthiest men in Danby Hollow," he says. "And God knows I'm not handsome. Or likely to change the course of Western Civilization. And I realize there are probably men out there who are all of those things—and would like very much to date Phoebe Laroque. But even an overweight glassblower with a civil service job is entitled to some happiness, isn't he?"

I've been waiting for this moment ever since he's mentioned the girl named Dover, but now I'm not ready to say yes. I want to say something that is neither *yes* nor *no*, but somewhere in between—

full of warmth, yet non-committal. Unfortunately, the occasion calls for a more decisive verdict.

Artie begins making his case again—and that's when I first hear the rumbling. A murmur that swells into an angry mechanical gallop. "Do you hear that?"

"Please, Phoebe," says Artie. "At least, hear me out."

I walk to the window and peer into the darkness. The snow has tapered to flurries and the HAZMAT team is rolling over the bridge in a squadron of heavily-plated vehicles that resemble armored personnel carriers. One by one, they stop in front of our tiny cabin and maneuver their way into a circle. I'm expecting a high-ranking civilian in a well-tailored suit to demand our surrender through a bullhorn—like in the movies—but the phalanx of identical creatures who emerge from the vehicles are dressed in futuristic white jumpsuits and say nothing. They enter the office in pairs, two approaching me, and two approaching Artie, and another to examining the lifeless woman. My coworker cuts short his confession. One of the men asks me a question, but I'm too dazed to hear it. "Are you alright?" he asks again.

I nod. "She's dead," I say. "She has four young daughters."

"What is your name?" the man asks.

"Her name is Zahida Khosa," I answer. "She's from Karachi. In Pakistan."

"*Your* name?" repeats the man.

And then, across the room, one of the white creatures lifts his visor, revealing a middle-aged male face with a bushy black moustache. "Chicken pox," he says.

Never has a voice sounded so decisive, so unequivocal.

"What?" asks his companion. "What are you doing?"

"It's *chicken* pox," says the first man—clearly displeased. "It's the wrong rash."

That's the cry that runs down the line. It's the wrong rash. *The wrong rash!*

Poor Zahida Khosa is still dead, of course. So is her father-in-law. And her family back in Pakistan will be arranging two funerals, not one. Her four daughters will have their lives cleaved in halves forever. Artie Kimmel is still staring at me over the dead woman's body, his round, hapless face waiting for words of hope. But the rest of the world is already moving on, changing channels, looking forward to their next Christmas Eves with their families. I could look forward like this too—I could spend my next holiday at my sister's house with Artie Kimmel at my side, but somehow I know I won't do that. It will just be me next Christmas, I suspect. Me and Jimmy Stewart and the ghost of Zahida Khosa, defending the borders until the last.

Coulrophobia

. . . .

My father fancied himself a shrewd landlord—he refused to rent to lawyers, the children of lawyers, even a college girl who "had law school written all over her"—but he bit off too much when he sublet to the mime. That was the summer after I turned eleven, when we lived in the dilapidated Oakland duplex that my father billed as South Berkeley in the real estate listings. The structure itself was an ugly stucco cube, topped with red slate. But it sat at the end of a row of once fashionable ranch houses and bungalows, in their first throes of gentrification, shaded by eucalyptus trees and jacaranda. The colorful hedgerows—hibiscus, thundercloud plums, bougainvillea—lent our place a false air of elegance, though you didn't have to look too closely to spot the cracked terracotta and chipped paint. After the computer science department terminated my father's graduate studies—a parting he blamed on politics and they attributed to plagiarism—he'd paid the bills by renting the other half of the duplex, the portion he'd been using as a storeroom and study, to a hippie-turned-clairvoyant who conducted séances in her kitchen. Aquamarine—that was her *nom de guerre*—was in her early thirties. She had childbearing hips and didn't seem to own a bra. Sometimes she sunbathed topless behind the stockade fence that bisected our backyard, displaying her generously-oiled flesh to anyone peering out a second-story window. Yet after only six months, our clairvoyant had the fortune to connect with her late grandmother, an imperious woman who insisted our lodger tend to her tomb in Newfoundland. The result was that the rooms stood vacant while my father and stepmother bickered over money.

My stepmother was for unloading the apartment to the first bidder. She was the breadwinner, after all—copyediting medical journals for five dollars a page. To her, every month without a tenant meant more evenings cuddled up with galleys for *Orthopedics Today* and *Colon and Rectum*. My father preferred a wait-and-see approach. He was content to pass his afternoons watching for his stocks to scroll across the bottom of the television screen, or listening to right-wing talk radio, until a sufficiently worthy boarder came a-knocking. *Think long-term, Sylvia,* he said. *Think like a man.* Yet not even my father's sexist barbs—to which my stepmother rolled her eyes back under their lids like a toy clown—could attract the uber-tenant. My father turned down one young couple, a Romanian oboist with a slight Czech wife, because they were a "baby-risk": *Kids trip on things,* he said. *You might as well tape SUE ME to your ass.* (My father was the sort of man who associated young children with window guards and lead-paint abatement.) Another couple, Mexicans, failed the "civil forfeiture" test: *One ounce of weed,* said my father, *the DEA puts us all out on the street.* When my stepmother protested that the Mexicans were avowed Jehovah's Witnesses— they didn't even vote, let alone smoke dope—my father snorted and waved her off impatiently. *For now they are,* he said. *But nothing is carved in stone.* . . . Several times that week, my stepmother threatened to move into the spare apartment herself: *I have limits, Gary,* she warned—shaking her hand horizontally at her forehead, as though to indicate the precise level beyond which she could endure no more. They were going at it like this *real good*, one steamy June morning, when the mime poked his head around the screen door.

"I'm here about the apartment," said the mime.

My stepmother made a sharp, forward motion with her head— her way of nudging my father toward the doorway. He cupped his fist in his palm.

"I'm sorry to interrupt," said the mime. "Your bell isn't working."

"You have to push harder," answered my father. "Like your life depends on it."

He led the mime across the tight concrete porch and heaved aside the warped rocking chair that blocked the door to the spare apartment. The mime eyed me curiously. His name—or at least the name he would later affix to the lease—was Simon Stillman. He was somewhere between thirty-five and fifty, his hair tinged gray, with large, almost helpless features that suggested wonder rather than sorrow. He sported worn dungarees and an un-tucked Los Angeles Dodgers t-shirt. More Red Skelton than Marcel Marceau. My father struggled to find the appropriate keys for each of the three door bolts. "Safest neighborhood in the world," he said to the mime. "Still, you can't be too careful with an empty apartment." Usually, I changed into my oldest clothes before we showed the place—"Go scrape a knee," was how my father phrased it—because that allegedly aided the rent negotiations, but I'd missed the opportunity. Not that I wasn't to be useful: "Turner," ordered my father. "Help the man with his bag."

The mime agreeably handed me his small leather satchel. At that point, I didn't yet know he was a mime—and I thought, given the satchel, he might be a physician who made house calls. "Take good care of that," said the mime. I nodded. My father pushed open the door and we stepped into the cool, stagnant interior.

The ceiling bulbs had burned out. We waited in the dusky entryway while my father went off for a flashlight. "Do you enjoy the dark?" asked the mime. His voice was nasal and vaguely midwestern.

I said nothing. I was a good, quiet kid.

"I enjoy the dark," said the mime. "It's very honest. Like silence." He stood arms akimbo, beaming like a human flower. "On the other hand," he added, diplomatically, "I enjoy the light too."

The door swung open and shut. My father blinded me with his flashlight, one of his favorite tricks. I shielded my eyes. "Gotta keep the boy on his toes," he said.

He steered our prospective tenant through the unadorned rooms, the walls stripped down to their sockets and picture hooks. Aquamarine had left behind a few husks of furniture—mostly threadbare upholstery—but not much. We were back on the veranda again, on the flagstone patio, when my father popped the question: "Are you, by any chance, an attorney?"

"No," said the mime, smiling. "I'm not."

My father slouched with his hands in his trouser pockets, waiting for more. The mime watched a magpie hopping along the adobe parapet, and said nothing.

"What line of work *are* you in?"

"Me?" answered the mime. "Entertainment."

My father lit up—his gotcha grin. "Entertainment, *television*?" he asked. "Or entertainment, *adult entertainment*?"

"Oh, no," said the mime. "Theatrical entertainment."

"That sounds somewhat risky," pursued my father. "Financially speaking, I mean."

"Maybe. It can be."

My father went in for the kill. "And your employer is . . . ?"

"Myself. I perform mime at the zoo."

Even at the age of eleven, I recognized this to be a fatal admission. He might as well have confessed to gun-running or pedophilia. Aquamarine, at least, had been a fortune teller *with a trust fund*. But my father looked up suddenly, like a man pierced by an arrow. My stepmother glared down from their bedroom window—her hair wrapped in a kerchief, her small, sharp features like blades. My father shifted his weight uncomfortably and examined the flagstones.

"You'll pay for the first month in advance?" he asked.

"Depends how much it is," answered the mime.

"Of course, that's a given," conceded my father. He appeared to have rapidly warmed to the idea of renting to the mime. "We'll go inside and figure out something reasonable."

"I do hope so," said the mime.

"I wanted to be a mime once," said my father, smirking. "But I talked myself out of it."

The mime did not laugh. "It's hard work," he said.

"I don't doubt that," agreed my father. "Mime is money."

Our new tenant retrieved his wallet from his back pocket. He redeemed his satchel with a five dollar bill.

Later that evening—after the mime and my father had negotiated a "fair" price—I watched around the front curtains as Simon repeatedly pressed the broken door bell. He had no way of knowing that the coils had rusted through, so he pushed with full force—as though poking out an eye. He tried using the tip of a broken branch, then the point of a baby-blue children's umbrella that he'd retrieved from the curbside. But when he finally gave up, he flashed me an unexpected smile. He looked satisfied, not frustrated. As though his efforts had confirmed what he'd known all along.

· · · · ·

After the mime's arrival, my parents' relationship took a momentary turn for the better—much the way a patient revives briefly before a relapse. They still bickered over little things, in-law visits, Fourth of July plans, who was to buy me new sneakers. But now they steered clear of the danger zone: money and sex. Although Simon Stillman hadn't laid out the first month's rent in advance—he told my father this sounded too much like a lawyer's ruse—the promise of a regular income lifted some of the weight off my stepmother's shoulders. She returned to aerobics. She let her long, strawberry-blonde hair hang loose to her waist. And since my father no longer referred to his bedroom as the ice palace, and to Sylvia as Nanook of the North, I imagine she did other things to his liking as well. Watching my father at the dinner table, during those first weeks of June, you could still discern the shadow of his irreverence, his youthful promise. He was once again the confident teenager who tried to gain admission to the San Francisco Aquarium while carrying a fishing rod, the brilliant undergraduate who'd been recruited to Berkeley as the next Alan Turing. Maybe that's what he'd been like *all the time* before my real mother discovered the caresses of her capoeira instructor, before the two women vanished into the ether. Or maybe that's just my wishful thinking. I guess we all try to imagine what our parents were like in childhood, in college—before life chewed them up and spit them out—and those long summer nights, when my father volleyed mime puns, offered the only portal I've ever had.

My stepmother must have shared my curiosity. One night, shortly after my father started programming for the phone company, she looked up from a kelly-green folder labeled Clinical Hepatology, and, apropos of nothing, asked: "What did you want to be when you grew up?"

My father flicked his cigarette ash into an empty Pabst can. "A computer scientist," he said.

"No, Gary. I mean before that. Did you ever want to be—I don't know, a mime? Or an astronaut? Or something like that?"

"Too long ago," said my father. "I can't remember."

"C'mon, Gary. I'll tell if you'll tell."

My father folded his arms across his chest and looked up at the sky. A few dim stars fought through the hazy orange glow of the city.

"I wanted to be a puppet maker," said Sylvia. "Like Gepetto." She drew her sweater over her shoulders. "Your turn."

"I told you. I can't remember." My father strolled to the umbrellaed table and took hold of the book I was reading. *Swiss Family Robinson*. He flipped through the pages indifferently and handed it back to me. "If your mother asked less questions," he said, "we'd be one big happy family."

"*Fewer* questions," interjected Sylvia. "*Fewer*. Not less."

"I tell you, kid," he said. "I should have married a mime."

"You mean a mute," said my stepmother. "Mimes can speak."

"As I said," said my father—but he sounded mellow, almost playful.

A similar mock-gruff humor marked his early encounters with Simon. The mime had repaired the warped rocking chair—his own father had been a union carpenter in Des Moines—and often relaxed under the porch eaves, reading. Although in many ways Simon defied the stereotypes of his profession, the same could not be said for his small personal library of thespian manuals and pacifist philosophy. He owned *The Pocket Gandhi*, *The Speeches of Martin Luther King*, Thomas Merton's *Seven Storey Mountain*. Also *Mime Time II: Another Book of Performance Tips*. My father, returning home from Pacific Bell with his tie loose around his collar, paused frequently to interrupt the mime's R & R with a bout of small talk.

"Whatcha reading?" my father might ask.

"This?" the mime would answer. "It's Dr. King's *Letter from Birmingham Jail*."

(Or he might say: *The Autobiography of Dorothy Day*, or Randolph Bourne's *The Development of Public Opinion*.)

That was the opening my father needed. "You sure I couldn't loan you something more your speed? Maybe *Silent Spring*? Or *All Quiet on the Western Front*?"

(Alternatively, my father might compliment Simon on his self-improvement efforts: *A mime is a terrible thing to waste*.)

The jokes proved relentless, but good-natured—and the mime took them in stride.

Simon's weekends were Mondays and Tuesdays. When he learned that my friends were all away at summer camp, but that we could only afford the free twice-a-week program at the community center—a god-awful experience characterized by forced swimming and long stretches of "quiet time"—Simon established a "clown camp" in his living room. *Just for me.* For three hours every Tuesday morning, he unveiled the mysteries of his little black satchel: setting powders that turned your skin to snow, "beard stipple" to create the illusion of facial hair. Simon wielded his brushes and sponges like a skilled swordsman. With a few slashes of a liner pencil, he could cut or raise his age by twenty years.

We did our work in dim light, illuminated by only the circle of decorative yellow bulbs built into the casing of Simon's mirror. Photographs and newspaper clippings were tucked into the corners of the frame: Nelson Mandela, Kermit & Miss Piggy, numerous snapshots of a young black teenager. The enormous reflective plate was the centerpiece of an otherwise under-furnished, almost Spartan dwelling.

"It's a show-biz mirror," Simon explained. "From my television days."

"You were on TV?" I asked.

"Here and there. Commercials mostly."

"Will you be on again?"

"I don't think so," he said, dabbing his cheeks with rouge.

"But it's possible?"

The mime put down his brush. Three delicate blue stars trailed away from the corner of his left eye. "I used to have a boy your age," he said. "He asked questions like that."

"What happened to him?"

Simon frowned. "He grew up."

(Later, I'd connect the grown-up son to the black teenager in the photographs. Adopted too late, said my stepmother. He'd deserted Simon for a career smuggling immigrants—and earned three decades in San Quentin when several day laborers turned up dead in a boxcar.)

The mime retrieved a derby hat and cane from his rollaway wardrobe. He set the hat on his head at a highly unreasonable angle.

"What will you be when you grown up?" he asked.

"A computer scientist," I said. "Or a mime."

"Good," said the mime. "Delightful."

And we might have continued at that pace, too. To an eleven year old, at least, anything is possible. But then my stepmother started miming, and Simon stopped paying rent.

. . . . .

One Tuesday morning—about a month into my "clown camp"—Sylvia found the mime and me under his locust tree, practicing characters. We stood facing each other, about five yards apart. I was an angel. Simon was a devil. Every five minutes we were to switch roles quickly, as though passing a rubber ball. When my stepmother appeared through the gate in the stockade fence, neither of us broke form.

"How are my two mimes?" she asked.

Simon didn't answer. Instead, his body—from forehead to rump—went suddenly angelic. His big eyes shifted heavenward. His arms rose slightly, their upturned hands opening like anemones. St. Gabriel, announcing John the Baptist, could not have shown such innocence. I responded with a curl of my fingertips, a fiendish flare of my nostrils.

"Not talking, are you?" said my stepmother. "The strong, silent types. Well, we'll see what we can do about that."

Moments later, Sylvia pushed open the gate with her back. The tray she carried offered lemonade, sugar wafers, cantaloupe balls on toothpicks.

I looked to Simon for permission to thaw. He transformed himself suddenly into a monument to hunger. Gone was his beatific purity, replaced by the desperation of a ravenous beggar. Yet other than a shift of his tongue—which now protruded puppy-like over his lower lip—it was hard to pinpoint how exactly he'd moved.

Even Sylvia was impressed. "Bravo!" she cried, tapping her hands together.

Simon stepped out of his pose. "Go on, young man," he said to me. "Eat. An actor cannot survive on mime alone."

He pulled a red Adirondack chair beside my stepmother's and settled onto the broad, flat arm. I poured extra sugar into my lemonade.

"That was remarkable," said Sylvia. "You have a gift."

"All in a day's work," said the mime.

"I didn't know mimes did that."

Simon smiled. "You thought we spent our time trapped in imaginary boxes."

My stepmother grinned sheepishly. "Maybe," she said.

"Would you like me to teach you?" asked the mime.

"It's too late for that," said Sylvia. "Besides, I talk too much."

"Nonsense. It will help relax you." The mime stood up. "Give me your hand." He took my stepmother by the arm and began to mold her body parts—shoulders, ankles, thighs. I was struck by his confidence, the ease with which he assumed this physical intimacy. Sylvia offered no resistance and rapidly adjusted into foundation stance.

That proved to be the first of many lessons. Simon taught my stepmother all of the standard illusions: walls, cliffs, spheres. They took turns hauling an imaginary boulder—which Simon later transmuted into an imaginary feather. They tugged either end of an invisible rope. The effect on my stepmother's mood was fast and sweeping: Overnight, she went from all nerves to nearly happy-go-lucky. She said mime soothed her soul. It made her feel—in her own words—*contentedly preverbal.* The time she'd once devoted to crossword puzzles and game shows was now spent under the honey locusts in the mime's yard, inventing a repertoire of lions, gorillas, teapots. Sylvia arrived at supper each evening as bright as a newly minted coin. She still corrected my grammar, often enough—but now she sometimes let slide an *irregardless* or a *very unique.*

At first, my father found my stepmother's new pursuits amusing. *It's every husband's dream,* he'd say, wryly. *All sex, no conversation.* Or *Silence, at last!* Soon, though, he grew prickly and resentful. Something essential had occurred in my stepmother's life, he must have sensed, and he wasn't part of it. So he complained his steaks were undercooked, that the bathroom needed scrubbing. *You'd have more time,* he griped, *if you didn't stand out there pretending to be a tree.* My father stuck his arms out haphazardly—mimicking a child's imitation of a tree—to emphasize his point. The truth was that Sylvia's cooking only improved with her new pastime. She even experimented with exotic recipes, *ceviches,* Ghanaian stews— for herself and me. The house was as pure as fresh laundry. Yet my stepmother endured these salvos with equanimity.

"Why don't you try it yourself?" she finally asked at our Fourth of July cookout.

"Because it's bullshit," said my father. He flipped a hamburger patty with his spatula. "All hoity-toity bullshit. Like men wearing kilts. If you ask me, there's something very aggressive—sinister— about these professional mimers."

"Do you know what you are, Gary? You're a coulrophobic. A man who's afraid of mimes."

My father accidentally flipped a patty off the grill. He kicked the lost meat to the edge of the patio with his sneaker. "If God didn't want us to speak," he said, "he wouldn't have given us mouths."

"Suit yourself," said my stepmother.

. . . . .

The following morning—after my father drove to work—Sylvia took me to the zoo. We rode a train, then a bus. Through the fog, she pointed out the Transamerica Pyramid, the Bank of America Building, Coit Tower. I'd been to the zoo when I was younger, but didn't remember.

First we saw the animals: the cozy meerkats, the oafish rhinos, the African elephants Maybelle and Lulu. (It was before noon on a foggy Wednesday. We had the giraffe house and the seal island all to ourselves.) As exciting as the wildlife might have been on another occasion, that day we were both going through motions. The sun had just cut through the haze, when we finally came upon Simon. He was in front of the food court. He'd attracted a crowd of about thirty, mostly teenage boys—they looked like campers from a church group.

The mime stood perched atop a black wooden box. He posed as a leopard, his entire weight resting on the ball of one foot. An oak tag placard reading PLEASE TIP THE MIME protruded from an upside-down top hat.

Sylvia wiped the moisture off a turquoise picnic table; I sat down beside her. Soon Simon became a locomotive. A butterfly. A tortoise. And then he performed the most fantastic feat—he fulfilled for us everyman's fantasy. Surrounded by onlookers, Simon did the unthinkable: He smiled directly at me and Sylvia. And he winked.

. . . . .

Shortly after that, money again became an issue. Simon had paid the June rent at his own initiative on the last day of the month. He'd knocked on the front door and had my father count the bills in broad daylight. The mime even requested a written receipt. But July rolled into August without a similar visit. (I later learned that it's far more difficult to evict a tenant who has already shelled out one month's rent.)

Rather than confronting Simon, my father avoided him. It was easier to vent his frustrations over supper.

"He's two weeks late," carped my father.

Sylvia sliced my lamb chops off the bone, cutting the meat into squares. "Relax," she said. "We're doing okay, now."

"It's the goddamn principle. Here it's fucking V-J Day and he still hasn't paid up."

"It's what?"

"Victory over Japan Day. August 15th," said my father. "You can't let yourself be taken advantage of like this."

My stepmother shrugged. "Nobody's taking advantage of me."

"Of course, they are. You just don't realize it." My father pushed his empty plate toward the center of the table. "You've been fucking brainwashed."

Sylvia poured herself a cup of hot tea. She held the tea cup at her lips, waiting for it to cool. She appeared to be considering her next sentence carefully. "Simon has been looking after Turner," she finally said. "And he's been helping me with my performance. Do you call that being taking advantage of?"

"Dammit, Sylvia," shouted my father, slamming his fist on the Formica tabletop. "Whose side are you on?"

My stepmother began to clear the dishes. "I didn't know there were sides," she said wearily.

"Well there are," said my father. "I also have fucking limits, Sylvia. I'm not running a homeless shelter. If he doesn't pay by tomorrow, he's out of here."

. . . . .

Three more weeks actually elapsed before my father confronted the mime. By then, Simon was also delinquent on the August rent. During those three weeks, my father—for all his bluster—appeared to take pains to avoid the encounter. Maybe he really *did* fear his tenant at some level. Or maybe he sensed something larger at stake. Whatever the cause, he arrived home earlier each afternoon—long before the mime returned from the zoo and settled onto the porch. And then my father lost his job entirely. *Reverse discrimination*, he said. *I can read between the lines.* Yet without the phone company income, we weren't doing okay anymore. My father no longer had a choice. He had to press Simon for the rent money.

He brought me with him, maybe hoping to play on the mime's sympathies. We found Simon dozing on his back patio. A thin book—Melville's *Bartleby the Scrivener*—lay folded open across his chest. Asleep, the mime's face looked slack and vacant. As expressionless as unhewn marble. On the flagstones at his side stood a bottle of merlot and a half empty wine glass. My father gave the mime's deckchair a hard, rattling kick with his boot.

"Look you," said my father, hyper-aggressively. "We need to talk."

Simon blinked twice. He rubbed his eyes with his fingers.

"I fell asleep," he said—as much to himself as to us.

"You owe me rent. Two months'.."

The mime nodded. "Yes," he said. "I do."

This admission appeared to catch my father off-guard. He took a long drag on his cigarette and blew the smoke into the mime's face. "When exactly do you plan on paying?"

Simon sat up, rubbing his hairline with his fingertips. "Soon," he said.

"*Soon?*"

"You know how it is," said Simon, deadpan. "Mime isn't *always* money."

My father stepped forward. I feared for an instant that he might grab the mime by the front of his t-shirt; he merely leaned menacingly over Simon's chair. In the process, he toppled the merlot bottle. The glass didn't crack, but red wine leached along the furrows of the deck.

"Soon," Simon said again—decidedly unruffled.

"Dammit," scowled my father. "You'd better."

He looked down at the spilt wine, then turned quickly and crossed through the gate in the stockade fence. I followed.

"Lazy shit," said my father. "I should have rented to a goddamn lawyer. At least they make a fuckload of money." He paced over to the barbecue grill and spit into the crabgrass. "Lazy shit," he shouted, much louder.

I wanted to hit my father, just then. "He gave the money away," I blurted out.

"What?"

"To the other performers at the zoo. The balloon artist, the one-armed juggler. The ones who don't make enough money on their own." I lowered my voice. "He said they needed the money more than you do."

My father glared down at me. He'd sweated through his shirt, and beads of perspiration limned the corners of his face. Behind him, two gray squirrels played cat-and-mouse along the roof of the neighbor's garage.

"How the fuck do you know that?"

"He told me," I said. I looked at the ground.

My father grabbed my shoulders, his fingers digging into my skin. He shook me hard. "Don't lie to me, kid."

"Okay, I saw him," I said.

My father's grip loosened slightly. I told him everything I wasn't supposed to tell: about our daily trips to the zoo, about how my mother did mime in the food court. It was all over in seconds. When I was done, my father shoved me backwards. "You'd make a lousy fucking spy, kid," he said. His eyes were smoldering.

He stormed up the back steps and slammed open the kitchen door.

"How long has this been going on?" he shouted.

"What's wrong?" I heard Sylvia ask.

"You and the fucking mime! The kid ratted on you."

"Please," begged my stepmother. "Simon will hear you."

"Who gives a shit if he hears me? He's the one who can't keep his cock to himself."

"Jesus Christ, Gary. It's not like that." (And as far as I know, it wasn't like that—not then.) I watched their distorted outlines through the frosted kitchen window.

"The hell it's not! How stupid do you think I am?" I heard the sound of something shattering—maybe porcelain on tile. "If he doesn't leave tomorrow, I'll throw his shit into the street."

"You do that," shouted my stepmother, "I'm leaving."

After that, silence. I can still imagine them glaring at each other—at a total impasse, with nothing left to say. Then a door slammed. And another. When I finally sneaked back into the house around midnight, the lights were out and Sylvia was sleeping on the sofa.

. . . . .

My father—not Sylvia—picked me up from the community center the next day. He hadn't shaved and his halitosis was worse than usual. From his clothing, rumpled, improperly buttoned, rose a fetid stench of stale tobacco and unwashed bedding. "She says I don't communicate," he complained. "Can you believe that shit? She's run off with a goddamn mime and *I* don't communicate." My father started the car before the passenger door was fully shut. On the drive to the city, we listened to Rush Limbaugh predicting the Sodom to come if Michael Dukakis ascended to the presidency.

"Do you remember where your idiot mother goes at the zoo?"

"No," I lied.

My father swerved around a slow-moving Cadillac. "Well, you'd better."

We found the zoo teeming with visitors. It was a warm, dry Friday afternoon—a rarity for the Bay Area in August—and people were making the most of it. The lines at the sno-cone stand extended past the koala cages; every seat on the carousel was occupied. The onlookers around the polar bear exhibit were so thick, you could hardly see through to the ice. When we arrived at the food court—my father periodically prodding my shoulder blades— it was standing-room only. My stepmother perched atop a wooden block at the foot of the mermaid-shaped fountain. Her pose was that of a sprinting deer. Around her milled teenage lovers, campers and counselors in matching t-shirts, a gaggle of overweight women enjoying ice cream. At the opposite end of the plaza, a larger crowd had gathered to watch Simon Stillman.

My father pushed through the crowd to Sylvia. She was bare-foot. In front of her lay a naugahyde tote bag, brimming with cash. A cardboard sign beside the bag read: *Mime Over Matter: If You Don't Mime, It Matters.* Below that: *TIPS*. Near Sylvia's tiny left foot lay a small paper airplane.

"Would you get down from there?" called my father.

My stepmother held to her rigid pose.

Several parents dragged away their young children. Others packed in to replace them. Few scenes draw spectators more quickly than a grown man antagonizing a mime.

"Enough of this bullshit," shouted my father. "Say something, dammit!"

My stepmother said nothing. Her gaze remained indifferent and fixed. More spectators magnetted toward the action, maybe anticipating a show.

"Please, say something," said my father. His voice softened and he added: "Please, Sylvia. Let's figure this out."

My father covered his eyes with his hand. For a moment, it appeared as though he might begin to cry. The crowd skulked backwards. This was personal now—dangerous. Far more than harassing a mime.

My stepmother remained silent and motionless. A lone grackle scavenged the asphalt beside her.

"Get the hell down from there, Sylvia," ordered my father, angry again. "You're making a goddamned fool of yourself." He raised his fist and shook it in the air, still shouting as the crowd retreated. I also inched away. Soon my father stood alone at the center of a growing circle, cursing, threatening, trapped behind the invisible walls of a no man's land that he'd created for himself.

Saluting the Magpie

Domestic upheaval: Our daughter, Calliope, swallows a penny. We've just celebrated her first birthday, and streamers still festoon the living room, when I hear Gillian shouting as though pirates have climbed up the fire escape. Not that pirates pose much of a threat on a balmy spring afternoon in Brooklyn, of course, but pirates are a useful shorthand for the lengthy list of unspeakable horrors that I suppose ought to flash through my mind as I fumble for the shower door and stagger down the hallway wrapped in a bath towel. Gillian has a knack for enumerating these horrors, which she does vividly whenever we drop the baby off at my mother's: feral dogs, and exposed wires, and kidnappers on the payroll of black-market adoption brokers. At the moment, none of these threats enter my thoughts. That's one of the differences between Gillian and me. What I'm actually thinking is: If Gillian keeps screaming like a crazy person, the widowed sisters living upstairs are going to complain to the landlord again. Of course, I know enough not to shout at my wife to quit screaming. In any case, she stops on her own once I've dripped my way into the kitchen, where she's bracing our red-faced Calliope on one knee and tapping the child's back with the heel of her palm.

"Thank God you're here!" Gillian cries—as though she has been awaiting my arrival for hours. "She swallowed a penny. Can you please do something?"

"Is she okay?"

"How can she possibly be okay? Jesus, Dave. She swallowed a fucking coin."

I don't know how my daughter can be okay. I'm a botanist, not a physician. But the girl is beaming from ear to ear, apparently proud of her deed. A cursory inspection of her neck reveals no unusual bulges.

I kiss Calliope's forehead. "I guess it will come out eventually," I say.

"You cannot be serious," snaps Gillian. "Nothing is happening *eventually*. All that toxic copper is leaching into her system *right now*. Not *eventually*. Am I making myself clear, Dave? My baby isn't a goddamn piggybank."

Not a choice time, I realize, to explain that pennies are made primarily from zinc.

"Okay, I'll call Dr. Frey," I offer.

"Here. Take her." Gillian deposits our child in my arms. "You know exactly what Dr. Frey is going to say. She's going to say not to worry." My wife picks up the wall telephone and adds, "*This* is why we need a new doctor. If Cal swallowed a live grenade, Dr. Frey would say not to worry."

I have no opportunity to defend our pediatrician before Gillian asks the operator to put her call through to Poison Control. Meanwhile, I tickle Calliope's tummy until she giggles, so my wife's distress won't alarm her. Three hundred sixty-six days have passed since this enchanting, feral creature entered our world—we are in a leap year— and I am still dumbfounded that her entire existence is half my doing. I am grinning, and Calliope is squealing, when the other responsible party covers the telephone receiver and thrusts it into my hand.

"You talk to him," Gillian insists. "He wants to know about the penny."

I glare at her—trying to wish my eyeballs into harpoons.

A male voice with a thick Indian accent greets me at the other end of the line. "So you are telling me that your child has ingested a penny," he says. "Is that correct?"

"Yes, that is correct."

I can hear the man typing, probably one of hundreds of similar young Indian men packed into an over-airconditioned office suite or gymnasium in Hyderabad or Bangalore or wherever, fielding emergency calls from the United States on the graveyard shift. For all that I know, the man has never even *seen* an American penny.

"What kind of penny?" he asks.

"What do you mean: What *kind* of penny?" I fire back. "A penny."

"All right, sir. Do you happen to know the year of the penny?"

"No, I don't know the year of the penny."

"Thank you, sir. You are telling me you do not know the year of the penny. Do you know at which location the penny was minted?"

"Excuse me?"

"If you will please look on the front of the coin, under the date, you may see a letter D, a letter S, or no letter at all. Are you able to look at the front of the coin?"

I refuse to let myself become frustrated. The man is just doing his job. I imagine he thinks we Americans are incompetent parents for letting our daughters eat our money.

"The penny is *inside* my daughter's stomach," I explain. "So *no*, I do not know at which location it was minted."

A long pause follows. I suppose this contingency is not on the therapeutic algorithm used by outsourced Poison Control agents. The man confers with a colleague in his native language, his words fast and anxious, before returning to me.

"Very well, sir. You are telling me that the penny is inside the stomach of your daughter," he says—still ineffably polite. "Under these circumstances, I must recommend that you seek further medical assistance at a hospital."

I thank the man for his insight and hang up the phone, determined not to endure a Sunday afternoon waiting for a doctor. "Poison Control agrees with me," I inform Gillian. "Nothing to worry about. Kids swallow coins all the time."

"I could care less what Poison Control says," she answers, already bundling Calliope into her outdoor cloak. "We're going to the emergency room."

One might ask why a person phones Poison Control *at all* if one is determined to take one's daughter to the emergency room *anyway*. After eight years of dating and five of marriage, a man learns not to ponder such impenetrable mysteries. My wife's personal choices are as complex and inscrutable as the highly-prized collages she fashions from discarded grocery packaging. And will remain so. Not even love can decipher them; it can only embrace them.

I recognize that the penny episode has become my responsibility, even though the swallowing occurred on Gillian's watch. I'm so certain of what I'm in for, that the accusation, when it finally arrives, is almost reassuring.

"What were you *thinking*?" demands Gillian.

We're in the back seat of a taxi, inching up Flatbush Avenue toward the hospital.

I brace myself. "Thinking about what?"

"Who leaves pennies within reach of a one-year-old?" To add to my discomfort, Gillian leans forward and asks the turbaned cabbie, "Would *you* leave pennies within reach of a one year old?"

"You have a very beautiful child," the driver replies with diplomacy. "You are very lucky to have such a beautiful child."

. . . . .

The pediatric emergency room on a Sunday afternoon is enough to scare any would-be parent into permanent celibacy. Ailing children wait on mechanized cots, enduring bloody eyes and swollen limbs, while their restless siblings scamper around IV poles and beneath cardiac monitors with minimal supervision. By the time we arrive, all of the beds are occupied, so we're assigned to a gurney in a corridor opposite the triage bay. On the adjacent gurney sits a shirtless, obese boy, at the cusp of adolescence, who insists on flashing his abdominal rash to passersby. "It's painless," he informs us while his mother visits the restroom. "I looked it up on the Internet last night and I'm pretty sure it's syphilis." At the opposite end of the passageway, a maintenance crew labors behind a cordon of yellow signs, mopping away another patient's vomit. Gillian and I take turns singing "Bye, Baby Bunting," Calliope's favorite lullaby, for over two hours, until our daughter finally dozes off. Minutes later, the pediatric resident arrives to examine her.

The young doctor appears kind, but obviously overwhelmed. Stray papers keep falling from the pockets of her white coat. Also M&M wrappers. When she leans forward to retrieve them, tongue depressors and plastic otoscope caps tumble out of her other pocket. She smiles apologetically, but she looks as though she's on the verge of tears—a reminder of how thankful I am that I decided to study the physiology of seaweed rather than human disease.

"I'm sorry," she apologizes. "It's my first day."

"But you *are* a pediatrician?" demands Gillian.

"Actually, I'm a psychiatry intern," explains the young doctor. "We rotate through the emergency room. But we're well supervised." She touches my wife's shoulder to console her. "Now tell me what happened?"

I relate to the resident how I left my pocket change on the kitchen countertop and how Calliope transformed a penny into an hors d'oeuvre. "A 1997 penny, minted in Philadelphia," I speculate—for no good reason. "Manufactured primarily out of zinc."

Gillian throws me a suspicious glance. The resident nods sympathetically.

"We should get an X-ray," says the young doctor. "To make sure the coin's not lodged within her esophagus. If it's in her stomach, we'll just let it pass on through."

The resident presses gently on Calliope's belly, peers into her throat with a penlight. I could as easily have performed the same examination at home. "I don't think it's anything to worry about," she declares. "My boss may stop by to say hello and then we'll get her that X-ray. But I'm afraid it could take a little while. We're down to one machine." She looks at us nervously, as though seeking approval. "Do you have any questions or concerns?"

"What was your name?" asks Gillian.

"I'm Dr. Clampitt," replies the young doctor. "But you can call me Maia."

So we wait another four hours for an X-ray. Soon the overflow corridor is crammed to capacity and two orderlies slide another gurney between ours and the fat boy's. He shows his rash to the new patient, a four-year-old girl nursing a toothache. The child soothes her pain with cloth-wrapped ice, which melts quickly inside the crowded ER, and she keeps dispatching her bespectacled grandaunt to obtain more cubes. Later, the girl asks Gillian, "What's syphilis?" By the time they summon Calliope for her dose of unnecessary radiation, I'm ready to start swallowing coins myself.

Gillian accompanies Calliope into the X-ray suite. I purchase a cup of coffee from a vending machine and pace outside the swinging doors. An attractive brunette takes a seat on a nearby bench, and I find myself admiring her body out of the corner of my eye, until I suddenly realize that I am looking at Dr. Frey. Our pediatrician sports tight-fitting jeans and an angora sweater that emphasizes her physique. I am accustomed to seeing her in a long, sterile lab coat. Her eyes catch mine, and she greets me by name.

"My nephew tripped on a garden hose," she explains. She has accompanied her sister's son for his X-rays, hoping to speed the process. "Without the right connections," she observes, "you can wait here for days."

"I know," I reply.

I relate the afternoon's events yet again—this time revealing that the swallowing episode occurred under Gillian's supervision. I can't help thinking that, if matrimony were entirely a scientific endeavor, I'd have married someone much like Elsa Frey. Our pediatrician is even-tempered, eminently reasonable. She also enjoys gardening, I've discovered—unlike Gillian, who couldn't tell a radish from a rutabaga. And, it's only fair to acknowledge, Elsa Frey is very easy on the eyes. But romance *isn't* a scientific equation. I've been in love with Gillian since she cheated off me on a tenth grade chemistry quiz, copying the alkali metals and the noble gases, and I can't conceive of loving anybody else. When my wife returns from the X-ray suite with our daughter's tiny pink arms wrapped around her neck, she's as dazzlingly attractive as on our first date.

"Look who I found," I declare.

I feel that I've redeemed myself by producing Dr. Frey—like a magician who flubs one trick and then pulls off another—but Gillian doesn't appear impressed.

Our pediatrician instructs my wife to set Calliope on a nearby stretcher and she performs a physical examination of her own. A far more thorough workup than the psychiatry intern's cursory effort. She borrows a stethoscope from a passing medical student and has him listen to our daughter's chest as well.

"It could be absolutely nothing," she observes. "A one-time fluke. Kids like to put things in their mouths.... On the other hand, it could be pica."

The only pika I know are the chinchilla-like rodents we encountered while camping in Utah, but I don't mention this.

"What's pica?" inquires Gillian.

"Some children develop cravings for non-nutritive substances," explains Dr. Frey. "Chalk. Soap. *Coins*. Nobody knows why." She cleanses the stethoscope's diaphragm with an alcohol pad and returns it to the medical student. "Pica is the Latin word for magpie. They say magpies will eat anything. Goats of the sky, they're called." The pediatrician shakes hands with Calliope, then with Gillian and me. "It's likely nothing to worry about. Just don't leave any more coins lying around the house and she should be fine.... Of course, if she *does* have another episode, definitely bring her by the office."

Maia Clampitt returns with the X-ray results a few moments later. The penny has settled safely into Calliope's stomach, an opaque white crescent on a field of black. In other words, our field trip has been an utter waste of time, but I don't point this out to Gillian. In the cab, I'm actually feeling rather conciliatory toward her. It dawns upon me that we haven't spoken, in any meaningful way, since our arrival at the emergency room.

"Isn't there a nursery rhyme about magpies?" I ask to break the silence. *"One for sorrow, two for joy, three for a girl, four for a boy..."*

"What?"

"I had this British zoology professor at Yale—Dr. April—and he used the expression 'saluting the magpie' all the time, because in England a solitary magpie is bad luck, and saluting it is supposedly a way to protect yourself.... To claim your own territory.... But then some visiting students from Oxford told us that it's also an off-color expression for something else entirely . . . and now I can't think of magpies without thinking of Dr. April's pecker . . ."

"For God's sake, Dave," interrupts Gillian. "Your daughter nearly dies and all you can think about are nursery rhymes!"

I turn to face my wife, waiting for the next blow. I know that her anxiety has not developed in a vacuum. When Gillian was only seven years old, her baby sister squeezed under a fence and drowned in the neighbor's swimming pool. Although she never actually saw the corpse, she still has nightmares in which Dora's body, red and bloated, bobs beyond her reach like a candied apple. Sometimes, of late, her sister's cadaver flips over to reveal Calliope's face. So my wife's anger has a history. I accept that.

"I didn't mean to snap at you," Gillian says. "I'm just on edge."

She reaches over the car-seat, above our sleeping child, and squeezes my hand.

. . . . .

We've already childproofed our apartment—forcing socket guards into the outlets, insulating extension cords with electrical tape—but, after the penny incident, Gillian grows determined to rid our home of all ingestible objects. She removes the magnets from the face of the refrigerator and unscrews the knobs from the doors to the stereo cabinet. My plants are banished to the highest shelves of my study, as is the fish tank, while the TetraMin flakes I feed to the gouramis must now be securely locked inside an iron bin along with Gillian's art supplies and my anti-seizure medication. After seven days of constant scrutiny and scouring, our apartment looks as though it has been picked clean by refugees. Then my wife discovers one of my old guitar picks inside the piano bench and she bursts into sobs.

"Why don't we hire a nanny?" I suggest. "We can afford it."

Afford is a subjective term. Maybe what I'm really saying is that hiring a nanny to look after Calliope seems cheaper than the psychological toll of not hiring one.

"I don't want to hire a nanny," insists Gillian. "That would just be another person to supervise . . . another person who might accidentally leave her coins out."

"You heard Dr. Frey, honey," I say. "It was a fluke. A one-off. Cal hasn't swallowed anything else in a week." I climb down to the living room carpet, where Calliope kneels in her pajamas while smacking together a pair of large plastic rings. "You're not going to swallow any more coins, darling, are you?"

"She's not going to have a chance to," says Gillian—but I've made my wife smile. I have the habit of negotiating with small children and domestic animals as though they're capable of understanding, even though rationally I realize that they're not. Gillian always finds this quirk highly amusing. Once she caught me urging our Siamese fighting fish not to overeat, and we laughed about it for months. That was during her pregnancy, but it already seems like a lifetime ago. Now she joins us on the floor and starts buttoning Calliope's sweater. "Let's get her ready for bed," she says. Seconds later, she lets out a profanity-laced cry of horror.

"What's wrong?" I ask

"Look!"

She draws Calliope towards us. Our daughter looks fearful, but otherwise unscathed. Nonetheless, I assess her closely—as though searching for a hidden image in a cluttered drawing. Nothing. I sense that this is Gillian's version of a Rorschach test, and that I am failing miserably.

"Look," pleads Gillian. "She's lost a button."

I still don't notice anything amiss, at first. None of the buttons appear misaligned and I discern no visible gaps. Yet, sure enough, an extra eyelet scars the lower hem of the girl's sweater. I hook my index finger through the knit to satisfy myself that the perforation is not an optical illusion. It isn't. Two torn loops of pink yarn mark the site of the missing wooden disk.

"What now?" asks Gillian.

"Now we get her ready for bed," I say. "Not a big deal. Honestly, it's probably lying in her playpen at my mother's."

"She swallowed it," answers Gillian. "I just know she did."

"Okay, so maybe she swallowed it," I concede. "It's not a razor blade. Swallowing a wooden button isn't the end of the world."

"This is much larger than one button," replies Gillian. She is already removing the offending sweater. "Good God, Dave. Please tell me you understand that."

"Of course, I understand that," I assure her, although I'm not exactly certain what I'm confessing to understand.

"Well, show it then," Gillian orders.

"Okay," I agree. "What do you want me to do?"

Gillian looks me over, her pale brow furrowed. Maybe she is searching my face for a hint of sarcasm or insincerity. If that's her goal, she'll find none. "Why don't you tell Cal a bedtime story while I cut off these buttons?" she finally suggests—sounding relieved. "This is my fault," she continues. "What kind of mother buys her baby a sweater with wooden buttons?" My wife insists on apologizing to me, and then to Calliope, although our daughter appears far more interested in my impassioned rendition of Goldilocks. Every time I say, *"and this one was just right,"* I squeeze my daughter's nose, and she gurgles with glee. Soon she is sleeping, smiling dreamily. I cradle her tiny frame back and forth—awed that such an innocent creature can cause so much grief—while, in the background, I hear the blades of Gillian's scissors snipping through wool.

. . . . .

I phone my teaching assistant early the next morning and ask him if he'd like to lecture on "Lycophytes and Ferns." He jumps at the opportunity. I've only been out of graduate school for five years myself, but teaching—as much as I do enjoy it—no longer gives me the rush that it did when my only opportunities occurred while filling in for my mentor. In the same way, our family's frequent visits to Dr. Frey's office have lost their novelty. Eleven months ago, a bout of diarrhea or a fever of 99.8 was enough to have me calling our pediatrician's answering service at four o'clock in the morning. Now, although Calliope carries a penny, and possibly a wooden button, inside her gut, I am not even remotely alarmed. I suppose that I've come to view our daughter's health as inexorable, a certainty of the cosmos.

Dr. Frey shares office space with three other pediatricians in a low-slung stucco building across the boulevard from the hospital. When one steps across the threshold of the outer vestibule, a motion-sensor triggers a recording of "Pop! Goes the Weasel." Inside the waiting room, assorted toys lay strewn over the padded floor-mats like rubble.

The doctor squeezes us in before her first scheduled patient. She is wearing a shapeless lab coat once again, her auburn hair tied back—but I have trouble forgetting the curves that I now know lurk beneath her drab, loose-fitting uniform. I let Gillian do the talking, while I ponder our pediatrician's romantic status. She does not wear a wedding ring. Deep down, of course, I have no intention of cheating on Gillian. Even if I could. I'm more like the loyal employee who enjoys testing out his boss's office chair once in a while when his employer is away, even kicking his feet up on the chief's desk, knowing full well that he's never actually going to run the show. I catch Calliope reaching for the coffee cup full of pens on the pediatrician's desk and I stick out my tongue to distract her.

"That *is* a big button," I hear Dr. Frey say. Gillian is holding her thumb and her index finger approximately one centimeter apart. "But luckily the walls of the digestive tract have some built-in accommodation, so I wouldn't worry too much about the size. . . . You didn't happen to notice if she ever passed that penny."

"She hasn't," Gillian assures her. "And believe me, I've checked."

"Good. That's important," replies our pediatrician. "We want to make sure we have a running inventory of everything that's inside her."

My wife looks alarmed. "What do you mean? You're not saying we're going to keep letting her swallow things."

"Not if we can help it," agrees Dr. Frey. "But no method of prevention is foolproof. Children have a way of getting what they want." As if on cue, Calliope reaches for the pen cup again. This time, the pediatrician sidetracks her by producing a large orange sponge-ball. "That doesn't mean letting your guard down. Don't get me wrong. That just means accepting that, even with your guard up, she's bound to outsmart you some of the time."

"So there's no medication? No therapy?"

"Not for pica. If it is pica, that is," says the pediatrician. "Of course, twelve months is a very early age of onset. . . . In any case, the best thing we can do is hope that she outgrows it. Most patients do."

"And in the meantime?"

"Be vigilant. Put yourself in Calliope's shoes whenever you enter a new environment, always ask yourself what you would do if you were a twelve-month-old girl looking to ingest small objects."

"For how long?"

"Unfortunately, I can't give you a firm answer. I wish I could," says Dr. Frey. "Some cases last months. Others last years. . . . And in a small percentage of cases..." She waves her hand. "That's a long way off. Let's not go there," she concludes. "The bottom line is that the overwhelming majority of children like Calliope ultimately go on to lead normal, happy lives, so there's no reason to think she won't."

I'm tempted to ask Dr. Frey what percentage of *all* people lead "happy lives"—whether happy lives aren't by definition *ab*normal—but I recognize that she'd find such questions transgressive. Instead, I lead my family back across the waiting room, where a conclave of other sickly children has already congregated, their mothers worshipping modern medicine to the timeless strains of "Pop! Goes the Weasel."

.....

It's only ten o'clock when we return from the doctor's—too late to justify the commute to the university, yet still early enough for almost anything else. I urge Gillian to take advantage of my presence. Ever since Calliope entered our lives, my wife has had only two afternoons each week to devote to her compositions, while my mother plays babysitter, so she rarely has a stretch of uninterrupted work-time that lasts more than three or four hours. I'm optimistic that a full day as an artist will help her unwind. Secretly, I'm also thrilled to have my daughter all to myself. While Gillian fashions shredded milk cartons into a three-dimensional portrait of Picasso and Braque kissing, Calliope and I take turns pressing buttons on a machine that mimics animal sounds. Every time my daughter makes the donkey bray or the turkey gobble, a perverse part of me hopes that the widowed sisters upstairs will phone the animal warden. Mistaking a children's toy for a barnyard would certainly undermine their credibility with the landlord. Alas, after a few minutes, Calliope grows tired of synthetic oinking and mooing. What she'd much rather do is lick the machine's console with her tongue. As a compromise, I offer her a jar of Gerber's peach puree and a glass of cow's milk. That's about when our perfect afternoon of father-daughter bonding begins to unravel.

My wife pokes her head into the kitchen to ask if we've seen her grandmother's silver thimble. "It's always in my sewing basket," she insists. "I also can't find my jade earrings, and the zipper tab from one of my winter boots is gone."

If I hadn't known Gillian for thirteen years, I might take these concerns more seriously. But I'm aware that my wife hasn't worn her jade earrings anytime in recent memory, probably since I escorted her to her Barnard College formal, and I didn't even know that she owned a sewing basket. The reality is that, instead of working on her collage, she has spent the morning combing our apartment for missing odds and ends. "Don't you think we should take her in for another X-ray?" presses Gillian. "Just to be safe?" I am about to tell her that there is absolutely nothing to worry about, that our daughter may be the healthiest one-year-old in Brooklyn—the Jack LaLanne of toddlerdom—when Calliope vomits up the baby food. Then she starts sobbing and hugs her arms to her tummy. Within seconds, with a vigor that would cheer the most partisan advocates of female domesticity, my wife assumes the role of nursemaid and I am banished from the room.

I try to look in on my two women every few hours, but each time Gillian waves me away. I hear her drawing a bath for Calliope, helping the girl into a fresh set of dry clothes. The last rays of the twilight are already losing their grasp on the fire escape when my wife finally tiptoes into my study. Her face is ashen.

"How is she?" I ask.

"Sick. Her stomach aches. She needs an X-ray," replies Gillian. "This is a catastrophe waiting to happen, Dave. I'm not sure why you can't see that."

My wife sits on the arm of the leather sofa, toying nervously with her wedding band. I know she is waiting for me to validate her concerns—to concede that we are in the midst of a crisis—but I am hurting too. To paraphrase the late Dr. April, the time has finally come to salute the matrimonial magpie.

"I've had enough of this endless game of good parent, bad parent," I say, making an effort to keep my voice soft and steady. "I love Cal just as much as you do."

"I know you do..." Gillian interjects.

"Let me finish," I continue. "I love Cal. And I love you too. But that doesn't mean I have to stand idly by while you act like a madwoman. X-rays aren't benign. You do realize that, don't you? You keep worrying about copper leaching from pennies, but X-raying a baby is just a step below sticking her inside the microwave." I'm going to add that a trip to the emergency room exposes children to all sorts of pathogens, raises the risk of whooping cough and viral meningitis and God knows what else, but now Gillian is weeping softly, so I cut myself short.

"I can't help myself, sometimes," she says. "I know what Cal feels like. Some days I just want to run out into the street and start stuffing strange objects down my throat until I can't breathe anymore. Doesn't that sound insane?"

"Not at all," I soothe her. "It just sounds like you're under a lot of stress."

"But I've *always* felt this way," says Gillian. "Not about the strange objects, but about letting go. I never told you this, but once last year, while you were away doing field work, I was seized with an overwhelming impulse to run into the street and throw myself at the first man I could find." Her face is buried in her hands, her voice barely audible. "I wouldn't really do that, of course. But somehow the idea of it made everything seem so easy.... You must hate me, don't you?"

My wife is trembling, and I wrap my arms around her. That night, we make love for the first time in months.

. . . . .

Breakfast finds Calliope's retching a distant memory. Our daughter sits in her highchair, banging her spoon gleefully against the attached plastic tray. Gillian is also in good spirits. Without any prompting, she suggests hiring a sitter for the evening and going to the movies. I am jubilant. Relieved. I coast through the workday high on tranquility, raising past test scores for any student who asks and assembling a bouquet of exotic irises from the university's hothouse for my secretary. That night, we watch Humphrey Bogart in *The Caine Mutiny* at the Atlantic Avenue Playhouse, then share a carafe of red wine over pasta at our favorite bistro on Steinhoff Street. Gillian's interrogation of our sitter, an auburn-haired actress named Lauren, remains well within the bounds of normal parenting. The following morning, despite some reluctance, she even agrees to leave Calliope with my mother and stepdad. "But your mom has to promise to keep the ringer on at all times," Gillian demands. "None of their napping bullshit." So I kiss my glowing wife at the door, where she has already donned a paint-splattered smock, drop off my hale, peony-cheeked daughter with her grateful grandmother, and slide into my role as benevolent junior professor and mild-mannered botanist with unprecedented jaunt and alacrity. I catch my reflection in the subway doors—a bookish creature in well-worn tweeds, his briefcase on his lap—and I am content enough with what I see.

My reprieve proves short-lived. I have some advance warning, because Gillian has phoned my mother, looking for me, at fifteen minute intervals since four o'clock. When I arrive at our apartment, carrying Calliope on my shoulders, the living room looks like it has been ravaged by a cyclone. All of the furniture stands gathered at the center of the carpet, as though in preparation for painting the walls—or, the ominous idea visits me, in preparation for a massive bonfire. Gone is any effort to keep ingestible objects above waist-level. An open toolbox, its screws and washers gleaming, rests menacingly beneath the halogen lamp. Gillian sits in a bare corner of the floor, where the piano once stood, leaning against the exposed plaster. Blood drips from a gash on her left temple.

"I can't find them," she says. "I swear I've looked everywhere."

I don't doubt her. "What can't you find?" I ask.

"You'll forgive me, won't you?" pleads Gillian. "We'll get her an X-ray, and she'll be okay, and then you'll forgive me . . ."

"Of course, I'll forgive you. Now what happened?"

My wife explains that some of the safety pins she has been using on her Picasso-Braque collage are missing. "I've only used eighty-four on the canvas, but the box is completely empty. That's a difference of sixteen safety pins!"

Calliope starts patting on the top of my head, then slapping my scalp with her palms. I stabilize her leg with one hand and hold my glasses straight with the other.

"Try to think clearly," I say. "You don't really believe she's swallowed sixteen safety pins?"

"I don't know what to believe," replies Gillian. "The safety pins are missing. They had to go somewhere, didn't they?"

"But we've been watching her? Don't you think we'd have noticed if she swallowed a box of pins?"

"Who knows? Maybe Lauren let her guard down last night," says Gillian. "Or maybe Cal has been sneaking out of her crib."

"So what now?" I ask. "We can't take the girl in for an X-ray every time we're short a paperclip or a feather."

Gillian says nothing. She remains slumped in the corner, her knees drawn to her chest beneath the smock. Streaks of eyeliner coat her cheeks and a strand of dried blood connects her forehead to the corner of her mouth. I carry Calliope into the kitchen and return to the living room with a damp paper towel. Silently, she takes the towel and salves her wound.

"How deep is that cut?" I ask. "Maybe you should get it checked out."

Gillian shrugs. "That's the least of my concerns," she says. She reaches for my hand and claps her fingers around my wrist. I can feel the desperation in her grip. "One X-ray, okay? For my peace of mind." My wife's eyes are wide and hopeful. "Just once, Dave. I promise. After that we'll figure something else out."

I survey the chaos of our apartment, the collage of bureaus and chairs and household artifacts piled high like a monument to Conestoga wagons. Upstairs, the widowed sisters are playing big band music on their stereo, filling the entire building with the rhythms of Glenn Miller and Tommy Dorsey.

I nod. "One X-ray," I agree. "For peace of mind."

My concession triggers an unexpected burst of tears from Calliope. I set her down on the parquet and she crawls into her mother's lap. The sobs ebb quickly, replaced by a look of wonder and a gush of babbling. Then, after a clap of silence, our daughter utters her first full word: "*EAT!*" It is unmistakable. She repeats her only word over and over again during dinner, a mantra of abstract resolve, seemingly immune to all of the cow's milk and pureed fruit that we can muster.

· · · · ·

Gillian is adamant that the X-ray cannot wait until morning. They're *pins*, she contends—they could perforate Calliope's intestines. Somehow, the *safety* aspect of the "safety pins" has slipped her mind, but I don't belabor the issue. I'd rather visit the pediatric emergency room on a weekday evening, when the traffic is relatively light, than on a school morning, when every aspiring, underage truant will be flailing in the throes of hypochondria. I'm also concerned about Gillian's forehead, which it turns out she injured against the dishwasher door. When we reach the hospital, I urge her to have her wound checked out while I wait with our daughter—but she refuses. "I want to see the X-ray with my own eyes," she insists. "It's for your own good, Dave. It will keep you from having to hide anything from me."

"I wouldn't do that," I say—but we both know that I'm lying.

We inform the triage nurse that Calliope has swallowed a collection of safety pins, and she shepherds us into a semi-private alcove. A hospital gown and a cloth blanket lie neatly folded at the foot of a narrow bed. Two other beds share this recess, but at ten o'clock on a Tuesday night, they stand empty. On the wall nearby, a glossy poster warns against the early signs of dehydration. All around us, assorted monitors bleat their need for immediate attention.

Anticipating another lengthy wait, I've brought along the galleys for my article on morning glories and moonflowers to proofread. I spread my taxonomic charts out atop one of the empty beds. Meanwhile, Gillian smoothes Calliope's hair. Miraculously, the pediatric resident appears to serve us only moments later. It is Maia Clampitt once again. The would-be psychiatrist still has papers sticking out of her pockets, also a laminated card labeled: *Cheat Sheet for Pediatrics*. She looks as bewildered as ever.

"I'm actually not assigned to this bed, but I recognized your name on the chart, so I traded patients with Dr. Cobb," she tells us. "I've been reading up on pica all week. It's a fascinating illness—from a physician's perspective, that is." The young doctor removes a ballpoint pen from her coat. It contains no ink. She discards the pen, produces a second pen from a different pocket, and asks, "So what brings you in today?"

"She swallowed safety pins," explains Gillian. "Sixteen of them."

Dr. Clampitt frowns. "*Sixteen*? I could have sworn it said six on her chart."

"If you already know what happened," snaps my wife, "why are you asking?"

I feel genuinely sorry for the beleaguered intern. Dr. Clampitt's face suffuses a deep pink, and she appears poised to say something, but then she thinks the better of it and sets about examining Calliope. She speaks to my daughter as though the girl is an adult—asking permission to listen to her lungs, warning her before she palpates her belly—and that makes me like the young shrink all the more. I can't help feeling that Dr. Clampitt and I are on the same team—that we share the solidarity of knowing that my daughter is fine, that it's Gillian we're actually treating with this workup.

"Everything sounds good," the intern declares, tucking her stethoscope back into her overflowing pocket. "I'm not too worried."

"But you'll order an X-ray?" pushes Gillian.

"Honestly, I think it's overkill," replies Dr. Clampitt. "She had one last week. But if it will make you sleep better..."

"It will," says Gillian.

"Thank you, doctor," I add. "We really do appreciate it."

So once again, my wife accompanies our daughter into the radiology suite while I purchase coffee from a vending machine. I scan the benches opposite the swinging doors, hoping to see Dr. Frey once more, but the only occupant this evening is a bearded maintenance worker napping away his break. I glance at my watch. It is already after midnight. My teaching assistant may gain yet another chance at the big stage. I'm debating whether I should call him now, or wait until the morning, when my family returns. While Calliope was being imaged, someone had bandaged my wife's forehead. Gauze now surrounds her skull like a headband. "I know what you're thinking, Dave," says Gillian. "You're thinking that this is a colossal waste of time and that you could be home sleeping right now."

"That's not what I was thinking at all."

"Then what *were* you thinking?" asks Gillian.

"I was thinking that I want to make sure my daughter isn't going to die from a pin puncture," I reply. "And *then* I want to be home sleeping."

That seems to be the correct answer—or at least an acceptable one. Gillian smiles and caresses my cheek with her palm. I cup my hand over hers, squeezing gently. Then we return to our secluded alcove to wait.

On our prior visit to the ER, it required only twenty minutes to read my daughter's X-ray, so nothing prepares us for an hour-long delay. When Dr. Clampitt finally arrives, I'm expecting her to announce Calliope's clean bill of health. Instead, she says that Dr. Budge, the attending pediatrician, wishes to speak with us. "I'm sure it's nothing," I promise Gillian. "They probably lost the X-ray." But when Dr. Budge finally appears, sporting a bowtie beneath his hard grimace and hangdog jowls, he does not strike me as a man who would tolerate the loss of an X-ray. Maia Clampitt trails him at several paces, looking as though she fears a firing squad.

"I want to show you something," says Dr. Budge.

The pediatrician steps to a nearby workstation and we follow. He clicks several buttons on the computer monitor and types in Calliope's name. Without warning, her X-ray blankets the entire screen.

"Do you see that?" the doctor asks—tapping the image with a bare tongue depressor. "And that? And that? And that?"

I don't need to be a radiologist to recognize that something is amiss. The distinct outline of several safety pins is visible inside my daughter's stomach, as well as numerous white slivers that I soon realize are other pins captured at lateral angles. But that is not the worst that the image has to reveal. Where last week there had been one small coin, now there are at least six of various sizes. Dimes? Quarters? Foreign currency? Also two opaque squares that look like dice, a bent paperclip, and what resembles a trio of children's jacks. And then there are several other small white silhouettes of unidentifiable household detritus: Thumbtacks? Marbles? Maybe the outline of an oblate wooden button? "Your daughter has been a busy young lady," declares Dr. Budge.

"So what do we do?" asks Gillian.

"Nothing," replies Dr. Budge. "We could put an endoscope down there, but the risk of perforation probably outweighs any benefit. Nobody ever died from walking around with a few pins in her stomach. But you've got to keep a much better eye on this young lady—or she will end up swallowing something dangerous."

"We've been trying," pleads Gillian.

"Well, try harder," answers Dr. Budge. "Strap her down if you have to. Pica is serious business. When I was in the navy, Mrs. Hertz, a midshipman brought in a three-year-old who had swallowed an incendiary bullet." He presses another button on the keyboard and Calliope's innards vanish from the computer screen. "There's only one treatment for pica, I'm afraid. Growing an extra eye in the backs of your heads."

That's all the wisdom that the attending physician has to offer. "Follow up with your regular pediatrician," he says. "Come back if she develops any symptoms."

· · · · ·

We return home to an apartment that is bare and grim. With all of the furniture heaped in the centers of the rooms, the place conveys the impression that it will soon be vacated. I plug in the table lamps, but the incandescent bulbs cast shadows that make the naked walls appear even starker.

Calliope has fallen asleep in the cab, but now she is awake once again. Gillian announces that she'll put out daughter to bed. *On her own.* So I begin returning the living room furniture to its proper place, trying to remember the precise location of various bookshelves and bureaus, but everything seems slightly off, or maybe it's just my imagination; in any case, soon the endeavor no longer seems worth the effort. Instead, I retreat into the bedroom to wait for Gillian. I cannot imagine how my wife managed to lug the king-size bed away from the wall, but I don't bother to move it back. I lack the energy. Lying on the unmoored bed feels a bit like testing out a new mattress in a showroom. In the next room, my wife's high-pitched voice croons "Bye, Bye Bunting." I doze off in my clothes.

When I wake up, several hours later, Gillian has still not come to bed.

I peek into Calliope's room. Our daughter rests on her back, a slash of light from the airshaft illuminating her neck and shoulders. She looks angelic. A warm evening breeze blows through the open window, billowing the drapes.

I find Gillian in the kitchen, seated at the dining table. A tall glass of milk stands in front of her, also a milk carton and a small mound of pennies. My wife glances in my direction as I enter, but says nothing. I'm still reflecting on what *I* want to say when she places one of the pennies on her tongue and draws it into her mouth. Then she sips from the glass of milk and swallows.

I sit down opposite her and reach for her hand. She pulls it away.

"I'm putting myself in her shoes," my wife says. "That's what we should have been doing all along. *Both* of us."

Gillian takes two more pennies from the pile and swallows one, gagging violently as the coin goes down. She places the other coin in the palm of my hand. It is a 1992 penny, minted in Denver. It weighs hardly an ounce, yet it feels heavier than a sack of lead against my skin.

Together, we watch the copper coin as it rests on my bare flesh, and I understand that we are both waiting for me to swallow it. That is what love is about, isn't it? Swallowing the ingestible. I am sure I will do it too—and yet I don't move. I can feel the muscles of my gullet constricting, my tonsils engorging with blood. I want to be the man who will swallow a roll of pennies for the woman he loves, but that man is no longer me. The throat of my life has already narrowed too far.

Fata Morgana

· ·

Josh had twisted his ankle climbing Hverfell crater, so Megan traveled alone in the jeep with the proprietor's son and the young couple from El Paso. She'd wanted to stay at the inn to nurse him—it *was* the second morning of their honeymoon, an occasion for something wifely—but he'd insisted she go it alone. *It's not every day you get to Iceland*, he'd said. *Besides, we're married now. We don't need to do things together.* (Secretly, Megan also suspected that he wanted to get her away from the sharp-tongued proprietor and her Christian of Denmark cigarettes.) So here she was, tracing the desolate coastal flatlands between Kópasker and Raufarhöfn, her eyes peeled for the daydream castles and the mountains that didn't exist. She cradled her camera in her lap, letting the breeze work its will with her hair. The white sun cut through the low-slung clouds in clean square beams as though passing through trapdoors from heaven. The light warmed Megan's bare arms. It was so perfect—the pure oceanic air, the broad-winged skuas flocking overhead, the baby girl ripening inside her—that all else, even Josh, seemed a distant mirage.

"So how'd you meet your husband?" called the El Paso woman from the backseat. At the inn, she'd introduced herself as Baby Ruth—like the candy bar, she said—but she looked as though she'd indulged in a few too many candy bars herself over the years, and

Josh had taken to calling her "Good n Plenty" behind her back. She worked as a purchasing agent for an ophthalmology laboratory, ordering pig retinas from slaughterhouses—or something like that. Megan knew enough about her to not want to know anymore. Several seconds elapsed as she registered that the voice from the backseat, slashing against the wind, was directed at her.

"Me and Josh?" said Megan. "We met in New York."

"New York," echoed Baby Ruth. Her husband—a round-faced, pudgy software engineer who wore khakis while hiking—nodded knowingly, as though New York were the answer to all of life's mysteries. His wife ploughed on. "*We* met playing tennis," she said. "We were both taking lessons. Beginners' lessons. Lyle and his buddy were playing on the next court, and I was just thinking what a good looking guy he was—and then his serve up and wallops me in the head."

"Accidentally," interjected Lyle.

Not hard enough, thought Megan. The woman's stories were like a second-rate sequel to *When Harry Met Sally*. Megan looked to their guide for sympathy, but he was focused on the narrow road. The proprietor's son, Freyr, always smelled of fresh tobacco. He wore a thick auburn beard, sunshades and a deer-stalker cap with the front brim pulled down—making it difficult to discern whether he was smiling.

"Another couple I know," said Baby Ruth. "They were sitting side by side at an all you can eat fish fry. Howard Johnson's, maybe. Or Red Lobster. Didn't know each other from Adam. The deal with this thing was that if you ate a certain amount, an ungodly amount, you got your meal free. So my friend's husband is a big guy, and he's putting away flounder like there's no tomorrow, and"—here the El Paso woman lowered her voice as though divulging a state secret—"then he throws up in her lap. *And she married him.* What do you make of that?"

Megan scanned the horizon for the imaginary summits. "I don't know," she said. "I can't eat fish."

The El Paso woman waited for more. Maybe a reference to the baby, or some horrific seafood allergy. When none proved forthcoming, she described another couple who had met each other during a bank holdup. Megan imagined that Baby Ruth had asked countless newlyweds how they'd found mates before she'd hooked her own—feigning interest in their lives while subtly mining for strategy. She appeared to have amassed an extensive playbook.

"Look to your left," said Freyr. He eased the jeep onto the gravel shoulder. "Can you see them?"

They all abandoned the car and approached the edge of the precipice. Before them stretched the headlands of the Melrakkaslé-ttarnes Peninsula, a vast plain of marsh and sand and rock. Freyr Lárusson raised his flannelled arm and pointed seaward. "Pretty amazing, no?"

"Where?" asked Baby Ruth. "All I see are islands."

That's all Megan could see, as well. A long chain of volcanic summits scattered along the horizon. The distant water mirrored their crests, making the mountains resemble oil tanks, and giant toy drums and, in one case, an ocean liner with three large smoke-stacks. A lone dwarf birch clung to a nearby ledge. Otherwise, nothing.

"They look so real," said Megan.

"All an illusion," said their guide. "*Fata Morgana*. The arctic mirage."

Megan snapped photos at various apertures.

He handed her a pair of binoculars. Through the lenses, the archipelago loomed all the more convincing.

"A few years back, one guy refused to believe me," said Freyr. "He rented a speedboat in Húsavík to prove me wrong." The guide shrugged. "They have explorers' maps in the National Museum of whole mountain ranges that aren't there."

The El Paso couple took turns posing for photographs. Then they recruited Freyr to immortalize them both. While they posed, he fished into his jacket and handed Megan a polished violet-gray stone. "Do you know what that is?"

She weighed the nugget in her hand. It was no bigger than a walnut, maybe the size of her baby's heart.

"It's a *sólarsteinn*," said Freyr. "A sunstone. If you look from below while you rotate it, the crystal will turn blue. That means you're lined up with the sun."

Freyr counted down from three and photographed the Texans.

"It's how the Vikings navigated at night," he said. "Jet planes use the same technology over the poles."

The proprietor's son had been raised by his American father on the Upper Peninsula of Michigan. He knew astronomy, geology, birds. Megan returned the gemstone to him, and his fingers grazed her palm. She realized, suddenly, that he was flirting.

Meanwhile, the El Paso couple had taken shelter in the jeep. They sat with their arms folded across their chests, looking vaguely impatient. Megan considered pausing to photograph a stand of blue lupin, but decided against it. She followed the guide over the rolling alpine tufts. She felt exposed, shaken.

"A penny for your thoughts," said Freyr.

The ordeal of the last two days had screwed with Megan's judgment. She wondered how open she should be.

"Honestly," she finally said. "I'm dying for a cigarette."

. . . . .

"It's like ending the romance of your life," Josh warned. "Worse. It's like ending it on your honeymoon."

That had been three years earlier. Megan had returned to New York from Amsterdam to look after her newly widowed mother. It was springtime. Ferns and lilacs burgeoned in the community garden, and each morning Megan awoke to find a canopy of crab apple blossoms strewn across her stoop. The entire city seemed lush, and green, and shrouded in moisture, the maple branches bent low as though weighed down by her step-father's death. Megan's mother proved beyond consolation. She'd once been an old sixty-five; she rapidly aged into an ancient seventy-two. Day after day, Cathy Van Dam sat at the window in the parlor and waited for nothing in particular. At night, she came to Megan's childhood bedroom and confessed her most intimate secrets. Her infidelities. Her sexual hang-ups. The infidelities of Megan's late father. Later, Megan referred to these episodes as emotional incest. They ended abruptly with a burst aorta. Only then did Megan lunge for control of her life—sell the brownstone, enroll in a photography workshop, sign up for the smoking cessation classes. This was her turning point. She could no longer remember the person she'd been before her mother's death.

The smoking cessation classes were sponsored by the Department of Health. The "students" sat in a circle, on folding chairs, in the gymnasium of a Brooklyn middle school—a room that smelled stubbornly of sweat and floor polish. Fold-out wooden bleachers lined three of the walls; the fourth, all glass, revealed a neatly-kept courtyard. A Japanese maple stood in the center of the atrium. One of the teachers from the school, a skeletal old man with an Einsteinian shock of white hair, chain-smoked there after dismissal. On the first day of class, Josh adopted the man as their mascot. "That's what smoking does to your skin," he said, deadpan. "That guy's only forty-seven."

Several students looked up, puzzled.

"A joke people," said Josh. "Work with me."

Megan smiled. She'd expected the leader of their cessation work-shop to be older, a battle-axe of the ward nurse or schoolmarm variety. Josh couldn't have been over thirty. She liked the fullness of his jaw and the slight hook to his nose—it made him look like a very handsome rooster—and the broad forearms protruding from his shirtsleeves. He was more attractive than good-looking, magnetic because he loved what he did. "Time to quit," Josh announced to start the session. "Mark Twain thought that quitting smoking was easy," he added. "He'd done it hundreds of times."

Megan laughed. She fell in love. She didn't quit.

She tried, of course. She loaded all of her smoking paraphernalia—matches, lighters, even a souvenir ashtray from her parents' trip to Indonesia—into a large black plastic trash bag and heaved it down the garbage shoot. That night—after the corner bodega had closed—she clawed through the refuse in the cellar to retrieve them. The next time she quit, two weeks later, the neighborhood suffered a power outage. She'd had nothing with which to light her candles—so she'd gone up the street for a book of matches and a pack of Parliament Lights. Megan agreed with everything that Josh taught in class—that each individual had her own path to quitting, that every failure was a steppingstone to success—but that was all beside the point. When Josh passed around a photograph of his own mother, who'd died of emphysema, Megan's first desire was to hug him tight. Her second was for a cigarette to calm her nerves. By then, of course, they'd been sleeping together for weeks.

"It's transference," Josh had said. "They warned us about this in training."

Megan sat up in bed. That evening the class had gone out to celebrate the last of their ten sessions together. They were both pleasantly drunk.

"Some people fall in love with their shrinks," he said. "You fell for me."

"Yes, I did. Hard." Megan reached under the sheets and squeezed his semi-erect penis to emphasize the point. She loved the faint line of black down that ran from his groin to his navel. "But I'm going back to Amsterdam at some point."

"At some point," he said.

"Soon."

She'd inherited a flower shop in the *Buitenveldert*, temporarily under the care of her father's long-time assistant. Unfortunately, Amsterdam was incompatible with Josh's other career—his *real* career—as a stand-up comic. *The Dutch aren't funny*, he said. *Did you hear the one about Anne Frank and the bombing of Rotterdam? Now that's not funny.* So it was New York or Los Angeles. But Megan had grown up with her father in Holland. She didn't see much difference between Manhattan and L.A.—it was like arguing whether one preferred to live under Stalin or Mussolini. You might as well have offered her Beirut or Baghdad. She often mused that New York and Los Angeles would someday merge, like the people and the pigs at the end of George Orwell's *Animal Farm*, into one seamless, trans-continental metropolis.

Megan walked naked into the kitchen. She fumbled through her purse, and returned smoking a cigarette. "It's after sex," she said. "It doesn't count."

"We'll have to scoop out your lungs," said Josh, "and repackage that stuff."

"Fuck off," she answered, gingerly. "This is my last one."

"Until the next one."

"Ever."

But soon she'd returned to Europe, where the air was damper, and smoke floated so delicately on the misty breeze. She'd lasted a full week. Then she broke down and phoned to say she wanted to keep dating—even if that meant, in the short run, long-distance. So they'd visited, and broken-up, and reconciled, and broken-up forever, and reconciled again—the uncertainty nearly killed her—and then they'd decided to get married and have a child. Megan wished she could explain it more logically, more systematically, than that. But she couldn't. It just happened. Like weather. Maybe part of her had imagined that marriage might offer a new clarity to their relationship, a license that trumped geography—even though another part of her recognized such hope as irrational. Did it matter? Here she was, thirty-one and married, *thirty-one and pregnant*, honeymooning in Iceland *because it was halfway*. (A joke turned serious. Neutral ground. *Like Reagan and Gorbachev*, quipped Josh.) And yet nothing, *nothing*, had been resolved.

Or one matter, only, had been resolved: Megan had to quit smoking. For the baby. She'd been on the wagon for two days, since the moment they hit the tarmac in Reykjavik, two long brutal days. *Some honeymoon!* She could barely hold it together. How the fuck was she supposed to figure out anything else?

. . . . .

Josh and Margrét Angantýsdóttir, Freyr's mother, were relaxing on the concrete plaza outside the Hotel Heljardalsfjöll when they returned from the *Fata Morgana* excursion. The hotel had been built as a country estate by an eccentric shipping magnate at mid-century. It was modeled on the Churchill seat at Blenheim. (The two men had corresponded extensively, although they'd never met.) The shipper had imported sixty tons of granite from Aberdeen, Scotland, and Barre, Vermont, before the Second World War curtailed his project. Only one small wing of the manor had ever been built. The rest of the stone slabs lay strewn across the *sandur*

like desecrated tombstones. Or makeshift *chaises longues*. Josh sat
on one, his bandaged foot elevated on another.

"Did you see nothing?" Josh asked, grinning.

They were alone with the proprietor. Freyr had gone to refuel
the jeep. The El Paso couple had retreated to their room for a siesta.

"Absolutely nothing," Megan answered. "I even have pictures."
She straddled a speckled pink stone. "How's your leg?"

Josh leaned over his leg. "*How are you, leg?*" He turned to Megan.
"He says he can't talk with all that gauze in his mouth." Josh
stretched his arms behind his shoulders. "More important, how
are your lungs?"

"I want a cigarette," snapped Megan. "How much difference
can one damn cigarette make?"

Margrét Angantýsdóttir poured Megan a cup of berry juice. The
proprietor dried her hands in her apron and said nothing. Already
she'd offered her opinions on tobacco: Hadn't she given birth to five
healthy sons—all over seven pounds—while puffing through three
packs a day? *Yesterday, the butter it is bad for you*, she'd said, holding up
her palms in mock frustration. *Today, the margarine it is bad for you.
You Americans and your scientists! I say all things in moderation. That's
how I raised my boys.* Margrét served up platters of sheep's blood
pudding and something called *súrsaðir hrútspungar*—Freyr later told
them it was rams' testicles pickled in whey—but she made the concession of not smoking around Megan. It was mid-August, after all.
Late season tourists were nothing to be scoffed at.

Megan smelled the tobacco on her hostess. "I'll have a cigarette
and then I'll have an abortion," she sniped. "We'll make a new
baby later."

She meant that, almost—her brain was so addled.

"You're nearly over the hump," soothed Josh. "Another day and
all the nicotine will be out of your system."

Megan bit her knuckles. "Another day and I'll be gnawing the brass off the banisters."

"I told you we could try a hypnotist. Or acupuncture," said Josh. "You're the one who insisted on cold turkey." And she had, too—as some sort of bizarre, self-inflicted love-test. Josh reached forward and caressed her arm. "Just trust me," he said. "Have some blind faith. It'll be okay."

A solitary raven hopped across the barren yard. Megan squeezed Josh's hand tight, pressed her flesh into his wedding ring.

"We'll keep you busy tomorrow," he said. "I'll be up on my feet by then."

The proprietor refilled Megan's glass. "He hasn't anything that a supper of herring cakes cannot cure," she interjected. Margrét's hair was drawn back under a red-checkered bandanna. She was pushing seventy, but you could see that she'd once been beautiful. "Lyle is taking the Lumbergs into the park tomorrow. You will travel with them, I imagine."

Jökulsárgljúfur National Park. The Icelandic Grand Canyon.

"You have never seen such cascades," said Margrét. "From the icecap."

"What do you say, honey?" asked Josh. "I'm sure I can out-walk Good n Plenty, even one leg short."

"Jesus, I can't think straight," answered Megan. "We have other things to talk about, don't we? Isn't that why we're here?"

"We're here because I love you," said Josh. "But one thing at a time, honey. Smoking and babies first."

. . . . .

After dinner that evening—broiled puffin, turbot, sweetened *skyr* yogurt—Margrét and her son withdrew to the parlor for a postprandial smoke. Megan and Josh retreated up the grand spiral staircase to their suite. The dollar didn't go very far against the *krona*, even late in the season, so they'd been surprised at the luxury of the accommodations: working fireplaces, a four-poster canopy bed, a private Jacuzzi in the bathroom. The windows of the front room opened onto the sea.

Josh drew back the curtains, exposing the craggy slopes capped with mating auks and guillemots. "What time is it?" he asked.

"Seven o'clock."

"Seven o'clock," Josh repeated. "Only another month until dusk."

The August sun still winked over the horizon at midnight. It would be several more weeks before stars were visible in the night sky.

Megan slid out of her jeans. She sat on the bed in her under-pants, her white muslin blouse hanging open. What she wanted most at that moment—besides a drag on a cigarette—was to hide under the bedcovers and to escape into slumber. But the previ-ous night she'd learned (*the hard way!*) that it was impossible to sleep off her cravings. She'd awoken several times from tobacco nightmares, ghastly hallucinations that she'd been smoking while unconscious. In one—the most vivid—she'd set fire to the bed. Megan placed her hands inside her slippers. She clapped the soles together aimlessly, like an applauding cartoon seal.

"Can we talk now?" she asked.

Josh pulled shut the drapes. He hobbled across the carpet and pulled forward the hassock of an upholstered chair, perching him-self on the edge.

"Of course, honey," he said. "What's up?"

Megan didn't even know where to begin. They'd been married in New York City to please his father—and she had a return ticket to J.F.K.—but her life, her friends, every single thing that she owned was in Amsterdam. Remembering the scent of hyacinth along the

Keizersgracht left her weepy. "We need to figure things out," she said. "Tonight."

"Sure thing," said Josh. "If you feel up to it."

That was such a Josh thing to say. *Sure thing.* So fucking glib. (He always preferred uncertainty to conflict—and that drove Megan bonkers.) But before she could gather her thoughts any further, a low moan resonated through the room.

"Do you hear that?" she asked.

At first, it sounded like wind blowing through the shutters. But soon the noise rose in pitch, a desperate rhythmic whimper like a child in pain. If it's meaning weren't clear enough, a man's voice cried out: "Baaaaaby Ruuuuuth . . . Baaaaaby Ruuuuuth!"

"So much for granite walls," said Josh. "It gives a whole new meaning to Good n Plenty."

The intensity of the whimpers rose.

"Baaaaaby Ruuuuuth . . . Baaaaaby Ruuuuuth!"

And then came the woman's answer: "Yes, Butterfinger . . . Like that, yes."

Josh rolled his eyes. "That is too good to be true," he said.

"I can't concentrate," said Megan.

Her husband dropped to his knees. He placed a palm on each of her bare thighs and spread her legs slightly, his touch soft and inviting. "What do you say we drown them out?"

"I don't know," said Megan. She wanted to, but she didn't. She knew that afterwards she'd be dying for a cigarette.

Josh slid her legs slightly farther apart. On the other side of the paneling, the El Paso woman shouted: "Butterfinger!"

Suddenly, Megan sensed the need for action. She stormed to the far wall and banged repeatedly with her slipper. Then she collapsed on the bed. When Josh placed his hand on the back of her shoulder, she shook him off violently.

. . . . .

Early the next morning, they drove to Jökulsárgljúfur. Megan rode shotgun. Baby Ruth squeezed between the husbands in the back of the jeep. The El Paso woman told the story of her mother's second cousin who'd constructed a makeshift pipe-organ out of water-filled champagne bottles. The girl he'd married could play "Some Enchanted Evening" by flicking her index finger against her throat. The two had met while busking on the Washington Metro. Megan was thankful for the woman's gabbing. It meant she didn't have to speak. She'd woken with an unpleasant coppery film under her tongue—smoker's patina—and she had nothing generous to say. While Baby Ruth chattered, they crossed expansive swathes of lightly-vegetated moor. Occasionally, Freyr pointed out an unusual geologic formation.

"I guess there's a lesson in all this," concluded Baby Ruth. "People have a way of finding each other."

"Like candy bars," muttered Josh.

"It's really a miracle," added Baby Ruth, seeming not to hear him. "With all the millions of men and women in the world, the right people always seem to end up together. Somehow."

After that, they rode several kilometers in silence. The jeep loosely followed the banks of the Jökulsá á Fjöllum along a rough dirt track, jolting over drainage ditches and washboarding. They passed through short-grass meadows and bleak lavascapes. Other than intermittent hikers—a sporty couple, an unkempt backpacker wielding a wooden staff—they encountered little evidence of human occupation. "Four hundred years ago," said Freyr, "this was the richest farmland in Iceland. Maybe in all of Europe. Then the *jökulhlaup* floods washed away the topsoil."

"Can we stop and take a picture?" asked Megan.

"Fine by me," said Freyr. "You're the boss."

Not that there was anything to photograph—just a husk of an abandoned barn and the rusted carcass of an adjacent tin shed. A split-rail fence warded off trespassers. Megan went through the motions of adjusting her camera. She had no intention of actually wasting an exposure, but she was feeling carsick and grateful for the break. Eventually her nausea passed—*Was this the onset of morning sickness?*—and she settled back into the passenger seat.

"All set?" asked Freyr.

She nodded.

Josh had been watching her efforts from the jeep. "No photograph?" he asked.

"The light's not right," she lied. "I thought I saw something that wasn't there."

Freyr turned the ignition. "Are you all right?" he asked her— probably too soft to be heard in the back of the vehicle.

"I guess so," she said.

"Just checking. You let me know if you're not."

But Megan felt better after that. At least physically. They made two additional stops on their drive to the waterfall—one at Ásbyrgi Canyon, the other to see the basalt honeycombs at Hljóðaklettar. The El Paso couple winded easily. Baby Ruth sweated a "V" on the breast of her t-shirt. During the numerous intervals while Freyr and Megan waited for the Texans to catch up, the guide courted her with Norse mythology. He told of the war god's airborne horse, Sleipnir, forming the valley with a footprint. Also of his own namesake, the spirit of springtime and fertility. If the proprietor's son wasn't a born storyteller—his narrative relied heavily on comparisons to "Hagar the Horrible" cartoons—at least he knew a damn lot. But Freyr could also be inconsiderate: At one point, he abruptly walked off behind a basalt pillar to take a leak, and returned reeking of tobacco. Meanwhile, Josh waited in the jeep, skimming the tour book. He was useless without crutches, and conserving himself for the hike to the cascades.

It wasn't a hike, really. Just a short, twenty minute stroll over a ridge. (You could hear the thunder of the *Dettifoss* before you could see it.) But supported by a borrowed Canadian crutch—a deceased cousin of Freyr's had once had a hip replaced—Josh's walking proved painstaking and methodical. Twice, he nearly lost his balance and clutched for Megan's arm. When they finally arrived at the falls, their guide and the Texans had already disappeared far up the bank.

They both wore waterproof parkas, but the spray nearly blinded them. Josh shielded his face with his hand. "Did you bring your barrel?" he said.

Megan positioned herself a safe distance from the edge. There was no guard rail. The humid air made her blood grieve for nicotine.

"Where are we going?" she asked.

She had to raise her voice to speak over the cataracts.

"What's that, honey?"

Josh turned to face her, his back to the water.

"Where are we going?" she repeated. "Next week, I mean. *After all this.*"

He met her with a calm and innocent smile. "Back to New York, I guess."

"And then?"

"And then we'll figure things out."

Megan felt her eyes moisten, aided by the driving rain of the *Dettifoss*. She had the sudden urge to push her husband backward over the embankment—to take them both into the churn of the falls.

"I can't take this," she said softly.

"What?" he shouted.

"I can't take this, dammit. I just can't."

Megan turned abruptly and scaled the steep, rocky path. Her husband called after her, but his words lost their shape in the spray. Halfway to the summit, she paused on a carved ledge and looked back: There was the man she loved, hopping after her, bracing one shoulder on his crutch and waving toward her with his opposite arm.

. . . . .

The guide found Megan on a mossy boulder, weeping. The hood of her parka draped loose down her back, and her hair was matted to her scalp. She sensed Freyr's presence before she looked up—and when he placed his hand on her shoulder, a soothing gesture, she did not pull away. "You sure you're okay?" he asked.

"Give me a cigarette," she said. "Please."

He frowned at her gently, his big black eyes full of indecision.

"It's *my* fucking life," she said.

"You're the boss."

He turned his back to her and lit himself a cigarette. Then he lit hers off his. "King's Originals," he warned her. "No filters."

She enjoyed a deep, rich drag. "Sweet heavens," she said. "You could lace them with glass shards for all I care."

The guide laughed—a generous, hardy laugh. He settled beside Megan on the boulder, and confidently locked his meaty fingers around her raw, limp ones. Freyr's company was like the opposite of a mirage—something that existed, when you knew it shouldn't—and she accepted his hand.

Hearth and Home

....

The vice consul's wife, Julie Ødegård, had been giving Norwegian lessons to the chimney sweep for nearly two months, but she still hadn't decided whether her feelings toward him were maternal or romantic. Favoring romance were the broad crossbeam of his shoulders, the arms built to wield Thor's hammer, the Viking hands fit for hurling bolts of lightning. She took pleasure in watching his big, soot-stained fingers drum the tabletop while he was thinking. She liked the ease of his smile, the boyish cut of his hair. Kurt Webb looked—there was no getting past it—like a Norse god. Yet the chimney sweep, although a widower, was substantially her junior. He was a young twenty-nine. She was an old forty-one. She was also conscious of the class barrier between them: Two decades of Scandinavian egalitarianism and *Janteloven* had crippled, but not crushed, her bourgeois instincts. All this kept Julie from knowing where things were going with Kurt—from knowing where she wanted them to go. She certainly had no *plan* to cheat on Adrian. And so long as she hadn't decided anything, Julie assured herself, she was doing nothing wrong. Why then, explaining the subtle difference between the verbs *skal* and *vil*, did she feel like Lady Chatterley?

They were sitting side by side on the sofa in the parlor. Kurt's language workbooks were spread out on the glass coffee table. The waltzing flames behind the spark screen cast a soft orange glow onto the geodes and kaleidoscopes atop the mantel. Julie marveled at the fire. Ever since Kurt had revealed to her the inner mysteries of the chimney—the intricate process for brushing the damper blades and the flue, why debris was cleared from the smoke shelf—she saw chimneys as fire-breathing mechanical clocks, serviced by skilled watchmakers. How had she ever dismissed them as hollow brick pipes? It was a wake-up call: There was so much she didn't know.

Kurt folded shut his notebook. "You're distracted," he said.

"Just thinking," she answered, smiling, "about the fire."

He turned toward her. She cradled her teacup for warmth.

"Jeg køjpte en presenning for deg," he said.

Julie grinned. "I don't think so."

"Ja," insisted Kurt. *"En god presenning."*

She enjoyed the chimney sweep's mistakes. They reminded her *not* of his linguistic shortcomings—but of his efforts. So different from most New Yorkers, who associated her adopted country with windmills and wooden shoes, or IKEA and Hans Christian Andersen. And years before, as the only student at Barnard doing an independent study in Norwegian, she had made her own share of foolish errors.

"You bought me a good *tarpaulin?*" she asked playfully.

Kurt frowned. He trawled his fingers along the brass trim of the table.

"I'm just teasing you," she said. "Present is *presang*. Not *presenning.*"

"You remember what you said about next weekend and being stuck alone?" Kurt said. The new ambassador had summoned Adrian to Washington to discuss the anti-whaling protests. "Well I got us theater tickets." Kurt spoke quickly. "Ibsen. *A Doll's House*. It opens on Friday."

Julie's pulse raced. She wanted to believe the invitation was harmless, innocent—but she saw the love-struck worry in the chimney sweep's winter-gray eyes. She parted her lips to speak, but didn't. Instead she looked to the fire for wisdom, and the portrait of Adrian's late father—bald, tuber-nosed, in full naval regalia—frowned down at her omnisciently.

"It's okay, isn't it?" Kurt added. "It's Norwegian."

It was hard to discern, sometimes, if he was joking. "Of course, it's okay," answered Julie. "*Et Dukkehjem.*"

"It's starring Dorothy Le Blanc," said Kurt. "Her big comeback." Some relief was visible on his face—but he still seemed unconvinced of her acceptance.

"Thank you," said Julie. "A night at the theater. How did you guess that was exactly what I needed?"

And it was, too. But she needed Bernard Shaw, *The Wild Duck*, Rodgers & Hammerstein. Anything light and frivolous. The idea of the young widower taking her to see *Et Dukkehjem* sent a flutter of dread through Julie's abdomen. Instantly, she thought of what she'd tell Adrian—*if* she'd tell Adrian. As soon as she thought *if*, she understood how attached she was, how deeply Kurt had burrowed under her skin. All that can-do optimism and those clean good looks had finally gotten to her. She didn't know whether she still possessed the strength to resist.

· · · · ·

Julie's "un-affair"—that's how she'd begun to think of it—had emerged from the sort of bureaucratic foul up that one expected in Trondheim, not in Washington. Adrian had been reassigned from the embassy to the New York consulate at the same time that another envoy, a young information officer named Haugen, had been dispatched to a post in Minneapolis. Both couples had relied on the same moving company. The result was that Julie's furniture had been delivered to Eden Prairie, Minnesota, while she arrived in Westchester to find her new home decorated to the Haugens' rather spare '70s tastes. She'd fought bitterly with Adrian: Why did these things always happen to them? *And how could he stay so damn calm about it?* She surveyed her "surprise" living room—the chairs shaped like question marks, the sleek monochrome vases, the vast expanse of bare hardwood floor—and the futuristic purgatory rendered her desperately homesick. Adrian lit the log fire to appease her. He'd already left for the consulate—another anti-whaling protest was anticipated that evening—when the ash clouded back into the parlor.

She'd had to phone six chimney cleaners before she found one willing to make a house call on a Sunday afternoon. When Kurt finally arrived, an ambassador of blue-collar know-how in his scruffy overalls and steel-toe boots, the spent fire extinguisher lay on the Haugen's long black sofa, oozing foam onto the leather. Although the bay windows stood wide open, the curtains billowing, the room still stank pungently of synthetic chemicals. Julie's sleeves were rolled up, her bare arms stained with charcoal and wood muck. She'd managed to stop up her tears.

The sweep dropped his paint-mottled toolbox on the hearthrug.

"You should have called the fire department," he said. "You could have had a chimney fire."

"I know," she said.

He surveyed the inglenook, jabbed the fire grate with a poker. Julie remained in the entryway, watching him at a distance.

"It's a beautiful house you have here, ma'am," he said. "I'd hate to see you lose your stuff for not calling the fire department."

"It's not my stuff," she said, sharply. "It's a goddamn accident."

The chimney sweep turned to face her. He stood patient as a fisherman with his arms folded across his chest. "You've had a rough day, ma'am," he said. "Why don't I come back tomorrow and we'll get that damper open for you."

"*Now!*" shouted Julie. "I'm sorry, I mean—Oh God. *Just please do it now.*"

And then she was sobbing again, her control ebbing and flowing, until somehow he was sitting beside her while she sipped a cup of hot cocoa. "I'm not usually like this," she explained. "It's the smoke," she added. "And the whales."

"The smoke, I know," he said.

So she told him about the whales. She told him about the minke slaughter and her ongoing battle with Adrian and about how she'd wanted him to resign from the service. She told him about being pelted with tomatoes and eggs by PETA, bottles and stones by Greenpeace. Then she told him about living divided between countries, about missing and despising America, of how free-thinking and decent and utterly suffocating she'd found life in Trondheim. Trondheim: Europe's most enlightened fishbowl. Julie was struck by the speed with which she opened up. In Norway, intimacy almost always arose gradually. But in the states, connections could be sudden and furious—maybe because they were so few and far between. It took the right circumstances, of course. The right company. Somehow she'd found that in the soft-spoken chimney sweep. His presence was comforting like a warm blanket. When he removed his work gloves to reveal a gold wedding band on one of his mammoth fingers, Julie suffered a twinge that was almost, but not quite, regret.

"You're such a good listener," she said suddenly. "I hope Mrs. Chimney Sweep knows how lucky she is."

"Mrs. Chimney Sweep was Maria," he answered. "And when she was alive, Mrs. Vice Consul's Wife, I wasn't such a good listener."

The chimney sweep stood up and paced alongside the sofa. He locked his hands behind his back; his boots squeaked on the walnut floor. "Are you sure you want to hear this?" he asked.

She wasn't—but she nodded. "You might as well pile it on the wreck."

"Okay, Mrs. Vice Consul's Wife," he said. "It's *your* wreck."

His story was shorter than hers. It sounded twice-told, whetted down to the essentials. He'd planned on following his father into the merchant marine, which would have meant months away from Maria, but she'd found an article on chimney cleaning. He still had the clipping somewhere: *So Long Mary Poppins: High Demand Has New Generation of Sweeps Chim-Chim-Cherooing*. It came from a home-oriented magazine she'd picked up at the dentist's. So he'd apprenticed to a roofer and learned the trade from scratch. He'd owned his own business before he could buy beer. The American dream. But then came Maria's strokes. After the first, she spoke like a foreigner. She said "plane station" for airport, "rain bath" for shower; it was beyond her understanding why bedroom and bathroom were syntactical, but "kitchen room" was not. Her lapses had been frustrating, but somehow endearing. After the second hemorrhage, Maria didn't say anything. She lay on her back like a hollow husk while the bed sores corroded her. When she finally went septic, it had been a blessing.

"What do you say when a twenty-three-year-old kid dies from an old man's disease?" asked the chimney sweep. His voice was hardly audible. "Maybe you don't say anything. Maybe you just wish you'd listened better when she was alive."

"I'm sorry," said Julie. "But why—?"

The chimney sweep shrugged. "After the first stroke, the neurologist said birth control pills. Later, he didn't know what to think. She'd been to Ecuador several times to see her grandparents. She could have picked up a parasite, he said." He pushed his hair up his forehead with his hand. "Does it matter?"

Julie hid behind her cocoa mug. "I guess not."

The chimney sweep turned quickly, his back to the open windows. "My great-grandparents were Norwegian," he said. "I've always wanted to visit. How hard is it to learn Norwegian?"

"I learned," said Julie. "I can teach you."

His eyes locked on hers. "Can you?"

"Everyone speaks English," she added. "But if you want..."

And so, two afternoons each week, when she was supposed to be editing her mythology manuscript—the manuscript, she might add, that was to be the definitive revision of Valhalla iconography— she instructed Kurt Webb in the language of his ancestors. It had all come about so quickly, so inexplicably. If someone had told her the story—that she'd developed a deep emotional intimacy with her chimney sweep—she would not have believed them. Maybe that was why, although she'd done nothing indecent, nothing that couldn't be revealed on the debate floor of the *Storting*, nothing unfit for children at a *fritidsklubb* or the *Humorslag* housewives, although these lessons might even be defended as civic-minded, as virtuous, she still hadn't breathed a word of them to her husband.

· · · · ·

Adrian phoned every night from Washington. He fed her morsels of gossip from the political life of the embassy: how the ambassador had introduced his Senegalese counterpart to *aquavit* and how, several glasses later, the African had offered Halvorsen his wife in return; how a high-ranking aide to an Alabama Congressman—one of the most reactionary members of the legislature— had been detained for soliciting gay sex at the Iwo Jima Memorial. They both painstakingly avoided the subject of whaling. That was because, deep down, they both knew that Julie was right—that behind all of Adrian's mulish bluster, he found the minke massacre as unconscionable as she did. They'd reached similar impasse on other issues. How often had her husband spouted drivel on the dangers of open immigration, on the Islamist threat to liberal democracy, ballyhooing positions he knew to be indefensible? Usually their political conversations ended when Adrian said: *I'll have to think things over.* That was his way of conceding. Afterwards, they made love. Or had phone sex, if Adrian was away. But Julie was now too stressed, too conflicted for that. She let Tuesday drift into Wednesday, Thursday, her theater engagement still secret.

Friday night Julie wore a strapless black dress, a pink tourmaline necklace, pearl earrings. She'd spent the whole afternoon preparing for her "un-date." She'd scoured the foyer tiles. She'd stashed her jewelry in the freezer, behind the frozen asparagus, in case the burglars struck during her absence. Later, she'd changed her mind about the necklace—the occasion demanded something more straightforward, maybe her silver cross pendant—and she'd had to defrost the chain on the radiator. She was standing just inside the closed front door, all teenage jitters, when Kurt's van pulled up.

"For you," he said. He handed her a spray of hyacinths. Tinfoil and a wet paper towel sheltered the stalk. Not exactly roses, but a gesture. "The first of spring."

"You didn't have to," she said.

He smiled, a bit sheepishly. "I wanted to."

"Well, thank you," she said. "You're all dressed up."

Kurt had traded in his neoprene smock and face mask for a sport jacket and paisley tie. "Us chimney men used to wear tuxedos. Way back when. The English butlers would pass their discards to us."

He escorted her to the van. Blocked across its flanks: *FLUE CLEANERS.* Below that, in smaller lettering, NO CHIMNEY TOO HIGH. Nearby stood a red brick chimney and a pick-axe wielding gnome in a top-hat. "I know he looks like a miner," explained Kurt. "My nephew designed it. In his *Seven Dwarves* phase."

The interior of Kurt's van smelled of glass polish and carpet cleanser. Also stale tobacco lacquered in verbena. Fresh from the car wash, thought Julie.

"Did they really wear top hats?" she asked.

"Yep," said Kurt. "And tails." He flashed her a broad, satisfied smile. "Most of the sweeps I meet don't know anything about the profession," he said. "Historically, I mean. It's sort of like how I heard this baseball player on the radio being told that he'd broken one of Lou Gehrig's records—times being hit by a pitch, or something—and he didn't have a clue who Lou Gehrig was. I just don't get that."

"You know a lot, don't you?" said Julie.

"I like to learn stuff," said Kurt. "Life is short."

"That's a good quality."

"I want to travel," said Kurt. "Norway, Rome, Madagascar."

"We were almost stationed in Italy. Almost."

Kurt reached for the gear shift; only inches separated their fingers. The van lurched over the Henry Hudson Bridge.

"The first thing I did when I chose chimneys," said Kurt. "I read *The Water Babies*. Charles Kingsley. I wanted to know what I was getting into."

Julie gazed out the window. "Do you *ever* know what you're getting into?"

Her entire life with Adrian had been a shock—both the good and the not-so-good. She'd just been some lovesick folklore major, after all, swept away by a visiting scholar. And there'd been the thrill of the scandal: of hooking the to-die-for young professor in the international relations program, of being remembered forever as the coed who'd eloped to Scandinavia. That they had similar values, similar interests—it was just dumb luck. A bull's-eye in the dark. But Julie's husband would never possess Kurt's far-flung curiosity, his wanderlust. Adrian knew some things, and he knew them well. History. Literature. Handicraft. If he was ignorant of others—chimneys, for instance, or sports—he lost no sleep over it. *Han fikk fred og ro*, he'd say: He'd found his peace and calm. Sometimes Adrian was her rock. Sometimes he was just plain infuriating.

"I read the play last night," said Kurt, apropos of nothing.

She'd been staring aimlessly out the window. "The play?"

"*Et Dukkehjem*." he said. "In Norwegian. With a dictionary."

They descended into an underground garage. The stench of rubber and exhaust seeped around the car windows.

"I have a confession to make," said Kurt.

His voice breathed gently through the pale yellow light. She considered reaching for his hand.

"I'm not Norwegian," he said. "I spoke to my mother last night. You'll hate me for this. My great-grandparents came from Copenhagen."

Julie let out her breath. She was thankful she'd kept her hands to herself. What caught her most off guard, she realized, was that Kurt had a mother.

"Does that mean no more lessons?" Julie asked.

"No. Of course, not."

"Well who cares then? Norway? Denmark? Whatever."

She laughed. He laughed too.

Adrian would kill me for that, she thought. But she didn't say it.

They crossed 50th Street and entered the Chaplin Theater like a couple.

· · · · ·

Their seats were in the second row, a stone's throw from the curtain. A small apron had been cordoned off at the base of the stage to allow for a grand piano. While the theater filled, the pianist dabbled in Grieg.

Kurt whistled under his breath. "Nice ceilings," he said. "I wonder if they're hand-carved."

Julie absorbed the intricate latticework, the gilded railings, the crystal chandeliers. Murals—she thought they were Biblical—graced the side walls. A family emerged on the balcony: a stooped man steering his white-haired mother's wheelchair, two adolescent daughters decked out for the prom.

"Thank you for this," said Julie.

Kurt closed his playbill. "Are you happy?" he asked.

Julie nodded. She feared she was blushing.

She'd told Kurt that she'd seen *A Doll's House* only a few times, but the true figure was closer to a few dozen. She'd attended classical performances and avant-garde performances. She'd seen all the men played by midgets. She'd seen all the women played by men. Shortly after her marriage, when they'd been stationed in Vancouver, she'd seen Torvald and Nora cast as a blind couple. The actors had sported dark glasses and been led around by Labrador retrievers. They'd edited the script so that Nora's rejected suitor, Dr. Rank, practiced ophthalmology. The following year, in Barcelona, she'd had to endure *Peer Gynt* in Catalan. That was the Norwegian expatriate's albatross: Wherever you went, whomever you befriended—Americans, Canadians, Spaniards—they all took you to Ibsen. Never Shakespeare. Never Brecht. Not even Strindberg. And should Adrian ever displease the Foreign Ministry—an admittedly unlikely occurrence—Julie anticipated hearing *Hedda Gabler* in Wolof or *An Enemy of the People* in Guarani. In Trondheim, of course, she'd not seen *Et Dukkehjem* even once ... although she'd been treated, over the years, to the entire oeuvre of Gilbert and Sullivan.

Julie glanced at her watch. It was after eight. A tremor of anticipation swept across the audience.

"Have you ever been *in* a play?" Kurt asked.

The question practically melted her. (It was precisely the sort of question that Adrian would never ask—because he wasn't imaginative *that way*, because he already knew all her answers.) Her track-record—*West Side Story* at summer camp, *Our Town* at college—seemed woefully inadequate. What she wanted to answer was: *I feel like I'm in a play right now!* Mercifully, they were distracted by a woman in an ermine stole, *a woman of a certain age*, sliding past them. Then the house lights dimmed. Applause erupted as Dorothy Le Blanc made her entrance; she lured the spotlight to center stage.

Kurt smiled at Julie—an intimate smile, like the caress of a hand. When Julie smiled too, she felt as though she'd stolen a kiss.

She tried to focus on the play—Kurt must have shelled out a fortune for the tickets—but her eyes kept drifting toward her date. It was *a date*, she realized. Calling it that made it so. *And she wanted it to be a date!* After so many years struggling to build a life among strangers, playing bridge with the diplomats' wives, canasta, pinochle, training herself to care about their genealogy projects, their aerobic walking, never having any true friends, wasn't she entitled to a small taste of pleasure? How had she never questioned it all before? *It was so unspeakably awful!* She'd complained to Adrian about the foreign service wives. The Norwegian matrons, although university educated, had practiced since birth to be ambassadorial hostesses. Their American counterparts, mostly Evangelical Christians, were eager and stupid. For the first time, Julie understood why Nora Helmer walked out on her husband.

"Free," Dorothy Le Blanc declared on stage. "To be free, absolutely free."

The actress staggered forward as she said the words. She sounded as though truly in agony. Who could blame her? She'd

had such a rough life—the incest, the abusive husbands, the alco-
holism. And now they said she'd been piloting when the speedboat
snagged the rocks—in effect, that she'd drowned her own children.
The poor woman looked forty going on seventy, her face a mask
of hard-set gutta-percha. "Many years from now," continued Le
Blanc, "when I've lost my looks a little, a time will come when
Torvald is not as devoted to me, not quite so happy when I dance
for him, and dress for him, and play with him." *And how many years
for me?* asked Julie. She peeked at Kurt. *How long before the unthinkable became the impossible?*

Julie no longer heard the play; she was listening to Kurt's steady
breathing.

Every passing minute was torture. His hand cupped the armrest.
She could easily have stroked the light down on the back of his
knuckles. How different from the crush she'd once had on Adrian.
Julie still remembered lying awake at night in her dorm room, the
pillow between her legs, begging God to let her have him. But with
Kurt—*well, she could have him!* His body wasn't unavailable, it was
merely forbidden.

The elderly woman in front of Julie whispered something to
her husband.

He was wearing a hearing aide. He cupped his hairy ear.
"What?"

The woman answered, too loud: "I think she's drunk."

Julie turned her gaze to the stage. Nora and Torvald were arguing about his business practices. Le Blanc wore a peculiar smile.
She kept fidgeting with her bra straps. Torvald was stout, jowled,
hideous. "Forget happiness," he barked. "Now it's just about saving
the remains, the wreckage, the appearance."

Adrian wasn't like *that*, of course. He wasn't Torvald Helmer.
Maybe he'd lost some hair, maybe he wore his trouser legs a bit

too short—but he respected her opinions, and he trusted her and, in his own way, he treasured the ground she walked on. Besides, she'd always made her own decisions. She could have traded in her mythological research for a job. She could have had children. *Dammit, she still could!* She was no Nora Helmer. The truth was that she didn't want to walk away from Adrian—she wanted Kurt *in addition to* Adrian. Like frosting atop a *lefse* cake.

A growing murmur drew Julie's attention.

"My Lord," gasped the obese woman to Julie's left. "She *is* drunk."

Le Blanc lurched forward, wielding her index finger like a pointer. "I have been performing tricks for you, Torvald," she bellowed. Her speech was slurred and uneven. She repeated herself: "I have been performing tricks for you, Torvald."

The actor portraying Torvald shifted his weight uncomfortably. "Have you?" he asked. He sounded doubtful—as though ad-libbing.

"I have," retorted LeBlanc. "Indeed, I have." A hostile, rabid grin hid her face like camouflage. She wobbled further toward the audience. "That's how I've survived," she rambled, swinging her arm wildly. "You wanted it like that. You and Papa have done me a great wrong." An aghast silence swept the crowd. "It's because of you..." said Le Blanc. "It's because of you..."

Julie looked at Kurt. He reached out, squeezed her hand.

And then it was over in an avalanche of shrieking: Dorothy Le Blanc had stepped straight off the front of the stage.

. . . . .

"Like a pirate," said Kurt, "walking the plank."

They were standing on the corner of 51st Street and 8th Avenue. Their initial shock had spilled into laughter as the absurdity of the spectacle sank in. Now they were casing restaurants—Afghan, Cuban, Vietnamese—still deciding whether or not they wanted dinner. A chill nipped the air, but Julie felt electric.

"I bet you've never seen *Et Dukkehjem* performed *like that*," said Kurt.

Julie hung on his elbow. "That's how they always perform it in Norway."

He glanced over to make sure she was smiling. "Is it now?" he asked archly. "Is that my lesson for the evening?"

Julie felt brave. "One of them."

They'd stopped walking and were standing under the awning of a fruit market, surrounded by bins of apples and mangoes and papayas. Kurt's face glowed tender in the pale light.

Kiss me, thought Julie. *Now. Kiss me.*

"I have another confession to make," he said.

She looked up and nodded gently.

"It's about when Maria had her stroke," said Kurt. "The first one."

Don't tell me this, thought Julie. *Kiss me.* She was suddenly aware of the honking of yellow cabs.

"I was seeing someone at the time," said Kurt. "Someone else." He brushed his hair back nervously with his hand. "You don't think less of me, do you?"

Julie shook her head.

"I broke things off immediately," said Kurt. "You believe me, don't you?"

The boy looked so desperate, suddenly. A giant, helpless puppy.

"Of course I believe you," she said.

He leaned forward—and it took a moment to realize he was kissing her. Julie pushed him away gently.

Kurt drew back, confused. "Is something wrong?"

"Not now," said Julie. "I don't want that now."

The boy appeared crestfallen. "What are you thinking?"

Julie merely shook her head. She was thinking about Adrian, about what would happen if he suffered a stroke. He was forty-eight years old. He had high blood pressure. It was known to happen.

The wind stung Julie's bare arms. "Please take me home," she said.

She wanted to touch the boy's wrist, to comfort him—but she understood that no good would come of that. He was still going places, places she had already been. What she wanted now was to light a log fire, to share it with her husband. For a long, long time. Already she saw clearly that her encounter with the chimney sweep was the best thing that had ever happened to their marriage—because it would *never* happen again. And if, on occasion, the scent of creosote still made her body tingle, she'd peck Adrian on his hairless pate, and they'd draw their chairs closer to the fire.

Counting
· · · · · · · · · · · · · · ·

I.

The government paid me good money one summer to interview all of the single women in Lawless County, Arizona. Before that I'd had a part-time job canvassing for American Express, asking *Chicano* day laborers and long-haired college kids whether they preferred Karl Malden or Jack Nicklaus as the poster boy of iron-clad credit, so it wasn't much of a stretch to trade my future in plastics for a present with the American Community Survey. My wife raised no objections. She'd just announced her pregnancy, the inevitable end to our celibate winter and thawless spring, casting me into that pit of quicksand between suspicion and proof. Each time Charlotte winced I imagined the child carving a scarlet A into the flesh of her womb, doing from within what I dared not from without, until even a summer in the Sonora sounded preferable to passing my golden years counting to nine on my fingers. If she'd protested, I might have stayed. As it was, I transferred my allegiance to the Bureau of the Census.

We did everything in teams that summer. Suspecting that an earlier generation of census takers had fabricated their results, Uncle Sam adopted the buddy-system as a concession to Big Brother and we reported our data in pairs like children counting-off on a school

outing. My partner, Revolution Schwartz, lived up to the expecta-
tions of his adoptive name. He was a twenty year veteran, a zealot,
a Sixties drop-out who reinvented himself as a latter-day Moses to
enumerate the tribes of the desert. "The census *is* the revolution,"
he'd say. "The census documents the inequalities of post-industrial
society." Although I couldn't help using the old fellow for occa-
sional target practice, inquiring whether Siamese twins counted as
one person or two, even asking the single women if they wished
to alter their marital status at my partner's expense, we negotiated
the saguaro-lined back roads without too much friction. Schwartz
chided me that we were also surveying families and single men;
I politely reminded him to change his clothing. All in good fun.

We grew into each other like an old married couple and I began
to think that our adventure might continue indefinitely. Then we
met the woman who refused to exist.

II.

"County Lot 4512," said Schwartz.

"County Lot 4512," I repeated.

He eased our rental compact off the macadam onto a narrow,
gravel driveway and we lurched into the belly of the desert. The mer-
cury had dipped to double digits the previous afternoon, a veritable
cold-snap, and the strange shadows of teddybear cholla and creosote
bushes danced in the morning breeze. It was hard to imagine that
anyone lived in this wilderness, among the jackrabbits and organ pipe
cacti, yet a stone structure embedded in a jagged ridge confirmed the
entry in the county surveyor's log. An ancient Chevy truck rusted at
the end of the drive. White undergarments fluttered too brightly from
an outdoor line. Some poor fool did indeed inhabit County Lot 4512.

We cut our way across the sand.

"No power lines," my partner observed. "They're off the grid."

My eyes roved in vain for a name plaque or mailbox. "Fear not, comrade," I said. "Man can survive on revolutionary zeal alone."

Schwartz grinned while recording the address on his clipboard. His shirtsleeves flapped against his thick arms. "Have your fun, Boyle," he said. "If they're militia types, I'll wait in the car."

"Viva Zapata." I raised my fist.

"Screw you," said Schwartz. "Your knock or mine?"

As though his question had been heard from within the confines of the stone shelter, the door creaked open suddenly and we stood face-to-face with—for lack of a better description—*her*. She filled the small door frame and offered no place to look. There were her breasts, pushing against a tight cotton blouse, then her clear jade eyes and full lips, finally her legs most distinctive in their absence. She supported her entire bodyweight on two steel crutches and this vulnerability only added to her beauty. Dank, climatized air seeped across the threshold. In the darkness over her shoulder a heavyset man sat at a pool table, constructing a palace out of playing cards. The hum of the power-generator augmented our silence.

"Either we already have one," she finally said, "or we couldn't possibly afford one."

"We're from the Census Bureau," replied Schwartz. "The American Community Survey Project. We only need half an hour of your time, ma'am."

Her jaw tightened and one couldn't tell whether she was straining under her own weight or displeased with our company. Asinine thoughts raced through my mind: "Don't mind us, we're just doing a leg count" and "I was always more of a breast man myself." The figure at the pool table added a card to his castle.

"The Census Bureau," lisped the legless woman. "That's not possible."

Then she added, sweetly, "We'd prefer you didn't count us," and pushed the door shut with a rapid swing of her crutch.

III.

This was not the first door we'd had slammed in our faces. According to Schwartz, a self-proclaimed authority on the history of enumeration, the original census takers doubled as tax agents— a primitive effort by the rising bourgeoisie to undermine our inherently egalitarian purpose. Some people loved us, of course, that core group of malcontents guaranteed to welcome any official visitor. Homebound veterans saw us as sounding boards for their gripes with the government; elderly widows offered us photographs of their nieces and nephews. For a while, Schwartz claimed, the Bureau even refused to hire good-looking men because they unwittingly raised the percentage of single females in the population. Only the working world saw us for what we must have been: a colossal waste of their time.

"How do you like that?" my partner demanded. He thrust his hands into his pockets and withdrew them irritably. "'We'd prefer you didn't count us, she says. I told you they were right-wingers."

"She's a looker, isn't she?"

"This is going to be a case for the federal marshal," he answered. "I can feel it in my bones."

"So you've never made it with an amputee, have you?"

"Screw you, Boyle. This is going to be a marshal case."

I slapped my partner on the shoulder. He'd acquired the habit of invoking the law when he found our target attractive, a somewhat endearing compromise between his principles and his pecker. We never did call out the marshal, never even discovered if he'd be *willing* to enforce the census, because persistence and the threat of a fine always proved enough to break down the toughest customers. In her case, even these extremes proved unnecessary. When Schwartz raised his clenched fist to rap on the door, it swung open again of its own accord. The legless woman braced her back against the frame and beckoned us inside with a tilt of her head. We had just enough space to squeeze past.

Our eyes adjusted slowly to the interior light until we found ourselves in a spacious, sparsely-furnished room which walked that fine line between residence and roadside saloon. Mounted animal heads and black-and-white photographs lined the paneled walls, an axe hung over the mantelpiece, stained glass lamps dangled from the rafters. One corner yielded a dartboard and a potbellied stove resting on lions' feet. Another revealed a free standing wet bar. At the center of this bizarre oasis, the heavyset man stood transfixed before his card palace. His elbows rested on the cushioned rail of the pool table. He did not look up. Schwartz stepped into the room ahead of me and then retreated back into the entryway.

"My husband likes cool air," said our hostess. "It calms his nerves." She lowered herself into a mechanized chair.

"He also likes games," she added. "Isn't that right, sweetie?" The man's head moved slightly in agreement.

"He'd like to play a game with you."

Schwartz coughed into his sleeve. "I'm Mr. Schwartz," he said calmly. "This is Mr. Boyle. We're here from the Census Bureau. We're required by law to ask you a handful of questions."

I was unprepared for the woman's laugh—a sharp, high-pitched chirp which stopped as quickly as it started, as though she'd just heard a particularly off-color joke. It struck me that she was younger than she'd first appeared, maybe twenty-five at the oldest. "By law? What are they going to do? Draw and quarter me?"

Schwartz shifted his weight from one leg to the other without mentioning the federal marshal.

"Let's talk straight. We don't vote. We don't pay taxes. We haven't left this place once in two years. For all practical purposes, we don't exist. You can't make us answer your questions."

The woman lit a cigarette. She crossed the remnants of her legs and one of her stumps appeared beneath the cuffs of her shorts. "So here's the deal," she said. "If my husband can build a card house to the ceiling, you go home empty handed. If he can't, we answer your questions. It's not often he has an audience. Now what do you say to that, Mister Schwartz?"

Schwartz said nothing at first. He rolled his eyes in my direction and then traced the air from the pool table to the beams of the ceiling. "What do you think, Boyle?" he asked. "Shall we humor them and kill a few minutes out of the sun or shall we call in the federal marshals?" His tone—all amusement—suggested that the decision had already been made and he solidified our plans by settling into a nearby bar stool.

Our hostess wheeled herself into the entryway and retrieved a wooden crate from behind the door. She displayed the contents for me. Playing cards. Decks and decks of playing cards. "Only two rules, Mister Boyle. If one of you knocks over the cards, you lose. If you talk to my husband, you lose. You don't like being talked to, do you, sweetie?"

The husband added a roof to the third story of his castle and then shook his head decisively, exposing a thick jagged scar that ran across his cheek into the folds of his neck. His gaze remained focused on the cards.

"He can't answer you, you see," said the woman. "He had his throat slashed in prison."

IV.

I seated myself opposite our hostess at a battered folding table whose surface was coated with the overlapping rings left by previous days' drinks and watched the husband ply his skills. He worked slowly, methodically, placing each card with the determined finality of a stone mason and then stepping back to survey his creation. Perspiration frowned across his brow. Sometimes he circled the pool table while he paused; other times he dried his hands on a dish towel and re-dried them on his well-worn trousers. As the castle rose from five stories to six, I began to suspect there was a method to his gestures, some obscure mathematical rule which governed when he circled and when he dried, but the specific logic of his maneuvers eluded me. If I anticipated a circle, he wiped. If I was certain he would wipe, he circled. I briefly wondered whether this wasn't part of his game, some calculated ploy to trick me into asking him to explain, but that had to be paranoia. He was just some crazy ex-con.

That first hour proved the roughest. I desperately wanted to speak to our hostess, but I couldn't. I couldn't even look at her. Although I'm rarely intimidated by women and was once something of a ladies' man, her vulnerable condition and the sheer brutality of her circumstances combined to keep me silent. What could I possibly say? That I suddenly felt like a fourteen-year-old kid in her presence? That her life could be so much better if she ditched her ex-con husband and ran off with me? That I'd be willing to rescue her? Absolute nonsense. I reminded myself that I didn't mean any of these things, that this was a married women, someone I hardly knew, yet her lisping voice and tapered stumps attracted me against my will. She had nothing. I had everything to offer. All of my thoughts seemed either fanciful or shameful.

I'd just resolved to say something, anything, as soon as the husband completed floor number nine, when she shifted her gaze from the pool table and asked, "Can I offer you a drink, Mister Schwartz?"

"Why not?" answered Schwartz, stretching his arms over his head for a peek at his watch. "You'll be making us lunch too, at this rate."

"Yes," agreed our hostess. "And dinner."

Schwartz pushed himself off the barstool and paced clockwise around the pool table. It struck me suddenly that the husband always paced counter-clockwise.

I followed our hostess to the wet bar.

"We only have bourbon," she said. "My husband only drinks bourbon."

She filled two glasses and handed one to my partner. Then she rolled out to the center of the room and balanced the other on the arm of her husband's chair. When she returned to the folding table, the card palace had surpassed ten stories and I was still without a drink. Schwartz chuckled. I seated myself opposite her and pretended to ignore the slight.

"Can you tell me something?" I asked.

"We're out of bourbon," she answered, matter-of-fact.

"Okay," I said. "That's not what I wanted to know."

"And what *did* you want to know?"

I drew a deep breath. "I wanted to know why you live like this," I said too forcefully. "I wanted to know why you don't want to exist."

The legless woman smiled dreamily as though deep in thought and yet even at that moment I suspected she was delaying her answer for effect. "If you exist," she finally said, "you have to explain things, and there are some things you can't explain to anyone."

"Like being married to an ex-con?" I asked aggressively.

"Like not having any legs," she fired back.

Her eyes darkened and I turned away quickly.

"I'm sorry," I said.

She laughed. "Don't be," she said in a softer tone. "I prefer it this way."

"You like not having any legs?" I asked incredulously.

"I like not existing," she answered. "It makes life much easier. Being somebody is highly overrated. You know, Mister Boyle, sometimes I feel like Greta Garbo. I think she would have understood me."

The husband grunted and we both turned to face him. His palace now rose twelve stories, almost a quarter of the way to the ceiling. His bourbon glass stood empty on his arm rest. A thin column of light peeked through the doorway of an adjoining room, animating the face cards, announcing that the sun had shifted to the southwest. Schwartz poked open the door, exposing a fold-out sofa bed and a bureau whose drawers were piled high with unsorted clothing. He thrust his hands into his pockets and retreated to his bar stool.

"This is ridiculous," said my partner. "Let's see how he works in the light of day."

"You do that," she answered. "Mister Boyle and I are going to go for a walk."

Her husband grunted again. It was difficult to tell whether this was a new addition to his routine or a particular response to his wife.

The legless woman tilted her head toward the front door and then herded me across the room. Schwartz looked after us wistfully—maybe an expression of jealousy, maybe fear of being trapped alone with the deranged ex-con. I didn't care. The legless woman wheeled to the threshold and turned for one final look at the rising palace.

"Mister Schwartz," she called out, "There's another case of bourbon under the sink. Help yourself. You may be here a while."

V.

We passed the afternoon in the shade of the saguaros. Our hostess—she pointedly refused to reveal her name—led me to a small alcove in the side of the ridge where she displayed her expertise on the fauna of the desert. Although I'd never taken an interest in the steady patter of the gilded woodpecker or the feeding habits of the cactus wren, she lisped the desert into a garden of tropical surprises. Did I know that javelinas suck the juice from prickly pear pads? That kangaroo rats can survive weeks without water? I let her guide the conversation, hanging on her every word, wondering whether she shared my romantic intentions. She expressed little interest in hearing my secrets, even less in revealing her own. "That's not what this is about," she'd say. "Why does everything have to have an explanation?" When the sun retreated behind the ridge, I knew an awful lot about the reproductive rituals of the yellow-shafted flicker and still nothing about my companion.

"What's all this about?" I finally asked. "Why the natural history? Why the card palace?"

"I like talking," she answered. "Sometimes you forget what it's like to have company."

I dug my hand into the cool sand and let it sift through my fingers. "I know, I know," I said, exasperated. "You like talking about the desert because it's there and your husband likes having us here because he wants an audience for his construction project."

"I like talking about the desert because it doesn't require an explanation," she retorted, "and for what it's worth, my husband couldn't care less about having an audience. He's happy enough to be alone with me. I'm the one who wanted you to stay."

She shivered as she spoke and rubbed her bare forearms. I dusted off the overshirt I'd been using as a blanket and tentatively draped it across her shoulders. The silent desert night encroached around us.

"I need to say something," I ventured.

I'd been planning the speech all afternoon, rehearsing my pledges of loyalty and devotion, bracing myself for the inevitable rejection. Now I longed to take her in my arms, to press her tortured body close to mine. So what if I didn't know the name to write on the marriage license? I'd lived with Charlotte for six years and left her as a stranger. If the legless woman didn't want explanations, so much the better. All I wanted was the comforting warmth of flesh against flesh, the reassurance that I could save her, that I could heal her, that I could free her from the mysterious ghosts which made such a beautiful woman fear existence.

"I think I love you," I said.

Our eyes met. My heart stood on tip-toes.

"I'm tired of talking," she said. "Let's go into the bedroom."

VI.

Our absence hadn't impeded the growth of the card palace. It now rose to within inches of the rafters, its base covering the entire surface of the pool table, part-Egyptian pyramid and part magic bean stalk. The husband had mounted a ladder. Schwartz circled the table nervously, crackling the wrappers of card decks under his feet, his entire body leaning each time the craftsman added a wall as though he could will the structure into rubble with his own body. The palace cast a long shadow in the waning sunlight.

Schwartz held a finger to his lips. "Don't speak," he whispered.

"Having fun?" I asked.

"Please don't speak," he pleaded. "If you knock it over, we lose."

His eyes were glassy, distant. He spoke as though the entire revolution hung in the balance. The husband added a dividing wall to his palace and the structure swayed ever so slightly, but didn't tumble. Both men grunted and then the husband paced while Schwartz wiped his hands on the dish towel.

I followed the legless woman into the adjoining room where she rolled her chair beside the bed and swung onto the mattress in one deft motion. Her body sank into the cushions. With the bedspread pulled up over her shorts, her injuries disappeared. She unbuttoned the top two buttons of her blouse.

"*Siamo o no siamo?*" she asked.

"What?"

"That's Italian," she said. "'Are we or aren't we?' My rehab instructor used to ask me that. I always thought it sounded sexy."

"But your husband?"

She laughed. "He won't care."

"You're kidding."

"You can close the door though, if you'd like. In fact, if you really love me so much, Mister Boyle, why don't you slam the door?"

"Do you mean—?" I asked.

She nodded and ran a playful hand though her long dark bangs.

"I am going to slam the door," I announced, making sure my words carried to the men at the pool table. "I am going to slam the door."

One quick swing was all it took. The entire house rattled under the force of the blow and then my name sounded from the next room, sandwiched between a salvo of expletives. Poor Schwartz, I thought. Long live the counter-revolution.

"I knew you'd do that," said the legless woman.

"A fool in love, right?"

"It doesn't matter though," she added. "You do understand that, don't you. He wouldn't have come in. When you've caught a woman once—at least the way he has—you're careful not to do it again. Years last longer in prison."

She must have seen my shock, my initial terror, her meaning cutting through me like a saw, for her own gaze combed the length of her body. My mind jumped to the axe above the mantle. "Do you understand now, Mister Boyle?" she asked, all the humor gone from her voice. "Do you understand why we prefer not to exist? Why we prefer not to explain?"

Schwartz pounded on the door, calling my name in anger.

"But why?" I asked. "How?"

The legless woman shook her head as though she pitied me.

"How, Mister Boyle?" she said. "Because we love each other."

VII.

The skies broke loose on our ride back to town. Distant claps of thunder gave way to the rolling staccato of ice on steel as bullet-sized hail pellets bounced off the hood of the compact. Lightning sawed across the desert sky, exposing our solitude, transforming the Lawless water tower into the hull of an abandoned ship. I'm certain this was the most remarkable phenomenon either of us will ever see in our lives and yet we said nothing.

Schwartz cleared his throat several times while he drove and I caught him craning his thick neck through the corner of my eye. He wanted to speak. I refused to meet his gaze. We'd already reached the outskirts of Lawless City when he shattered our truce.

"You can't do that," he shouted over the hail. "You can't screw with the census."

I denied him an answer.

"Girl or no girl, bet or no bet, we're going to have to go back out there tomorrow with a federal marshal." Schwartz raised a broad, hairy hand as though he might reach for my shoulder, but he didn't. It fell lifeless on the steering wheel. "Don't think I haven't been there before, Boyle," he said sympathetically. "It's not anybody's fault. Rules are rules."

"We're not going back out there," I answered, conscious of the chill in my voice.

"You know we have to," he said. "In the morning, you'll see, it will make the best sense."

Schwartz smiled hopefully, but I already saw him for what he was: a character I once knew, a piece of a story. What did I need with his rules? His sympathies? He'd fade into anecdote, soon enough, take his place beside Jack Nicklaus and Karl Malden and Charlotte and a host of people who didn't care about me one way or the other. All these people who weren't *her*. All these people who thought they really existed. At that moment, anything I shouted at Revolution Schwartz over a desert hailstorm was entirely irrelevant, so I chose my words carefully.

"You don't get it, Schwartz, do you? Some people matter more than others."

Silent Theology

· ·

My dead wife is dating Greta Garbo. It's that same spiteful streak Helen had when she was alive. She could have chosen Clark Gable or Humphrey Bogart or Gary Cooper—and instead she goes out and picks up Greta Garbo, because I once made the mistake of joking that I'd married the second sexiest woman on earth.

The two of them camp out in the living room after sundown. They foxtrot. They tango. They blast the old phonograph at top volume. Even with my earplugs in and my head smothered under a pillow, the vibrations of their heels on the floorboards keep me awake.

I try to block them out—try to forget that Helen ever existed—but there is no use. In life, Helen never argued. She mourned. I can remember returning after eleven some nights, having told her that I needed the solitude of the rectory to polish my sermon, only to find Helen at the kitchen table in her threadbare bathrobe with her pendulous cheeks drooping from fatigue and her eyes sad and reproving. It was a look of ultimate regret; the look of Lot's wife in the instant before her transformation to salt.

Helen never asked where I'd been, who I'd been with. She wanted to play martyr, to suffer for my sins. In death, too, she will not argue.

"For God's sake, Helen!" I shout from the top of the stairs.

She and Greta are no longer dancing. They are stretched out on the love seat, Helen's legs across Greta's lap. My wife ignores me. She draws a cork-tipped cigarette from her lover's silver case and blows the smoke out of the side of her mouth. The phonograph rattles the knickknacks in the cabinets, rocks the standing fan to a slow spin. I realize I haven't heard Tommy Dorsey in years. I try to lower the volume, but the knob is already in the low position. It twists and comes off in my hand.

"Can't we talk about this like adults, Helen?" I plead. I'm on my knees, in my boxers. Modesty seems irrelevant. The rough carpet near the coffee table burns my lower legs. "Talk to me, will you? Tell me what you want and I'll do it. Or just go away, for Christ's sake. Things can't go on like this."

Helen laughs. Not at me, but in good cheer. She appears as she did when I first married her, her long dark hair cascading down her back. Greta peers over her dark glasses and smiles seductively as though out of a poster. To my amazement, they kiss.

"It's a sin, Helen," I argue. "With a woman, it's a double sin!"

"Oh Greta, darling," says Helen. "I wonder what Chester's doing now. He's probably up at the rectory polishing a sermon again. And you know what, darling, I don't even care what she looks like."

"I'm here, Helen," I answer. "Right here."

I long for her to look mournful, sullen. Instead, she takes a deep drag on her cigarette and pulls Greta closer. I close my eyes and try to obliterate her. To will her away like pain. Then I feel the heat pan across my closed eyelids as she blows cigarette smoke into my face.

. . . . .

I try to tell my nitwit daughters when they come by to check up on me. They always come in pairs like mating sloths. The older one, the unmarried one, brings a worthless book and the younger one blathers endlessly about how happy she is that her father is still alive. She treats me like a photo album or set of antique candlesticks; I'm surprised she hasn't had me bronzed. Needless to say, neither nitwit offers any sympathy. "Your mother's cheating on me," I state emphatically, pacing the patio. "Do you hear me, girls? In the ground less than three months, and she's found herself a replacement."

Gloria folds shut her copy of *Messianics for Morons.* Anne toys nervously with her rings, her eyes expanding like the screen of an old television. Neither girl is pretty. Gloria has my features, down to the broad forehead and chiseled chin. She wears a cross around her neck that could anchor a ship. Flat-faced Anne, her eyes bulging, resembles Bette Davis on crack.

"Mother's dead," Gloria says.

"I know that," I snap back. I'm only seventy-three. I hate being treated like I don't know which end is up. "I'm not as senile as you think."

"Nobody thinks you're senile," Anne replies.

"Mother's dead," Gloria says again. Louder.

They exchange looks.

"She was here last night," I persist. "Or rather *they* were here. Your mother and Greta Garbo. Raiding the liquor cabinet and stomping across the living room. Do you hear me?"

"Jesus," mutters Gloria. She folds her arms across her chest; the bare flesh sags above her elbows. "That's what you get for watching so many movies. A vision! Hmph!"

Anne smiles at me. Then she turns to Gloria as though I'm not there and says, "Please, Glo, don't get him worked up. Watching movies is good for him. It occupies his time."

I feel the blood working its way into my chest. I want to lash out at them—my two nitwit daughters, this flesh of my flesh. I'd expected princesses. Grace Kellies, both of them. And *once* they were princesses: two April beauties with wondrous eyes gazing up from the front pew. At their father. At their king. And now I can't help despising them for their faded glory, for reminding me how old and ugly I've become. I was a king who'd expected princesses. And what do I have left? One daughter who thinks the second coming is going to occur during her lifetime and another who'd bob her head agreeably if I told her I was Jesus in the flesh.

"They upset the table lamp," I insist. "They tore the pages out of the family Bible."

"Of course they did," says Anne. She reaches for my hand, changes subjects like television channels. "Maybe you should cut back on your duties at the church and move in with me and Fred."

I determine to go into the house to tell Helen exactly what I think of her children. The delusion lasts only a split second. Then I remember that Helen is dead. Forever. I recall her spiteful grin, the vehemence with which she blew the smoke into my closed eyes.

"She tried to blind me!" I shout at my daughters. They lean toward each other in their deck chairs as though posing for a family photograph. They offer nothing.

· · · · ·

Six straight nights Helen relives the Jazz Age in our living room. I spend my mornings scrubbing dried lipstick off the champaign glasses, my afternoons watching *Anna Christie* on video tape. On the television screen, Greta says, "Gimme a whiskey, ginger ale on the side . . . and don't be stingy, baby!" over and over again. In the living room, she says nothing. She smiles, she flirts, but she is speechless. As though death has frozen her permanently in the silents.

I can't sleep. It's not even their racket, it's their presence. It's like trying to read while a stranger stares at you. I wander the house at night performing unnecessary chores: I clean the heads on my electric razor; I scrub the mould from the cracks in the bathroom shower with a toothbrush. Is this atonement? Is this precisely what Helen expects of me? Does she know that every beat on the floorboards brings us closer to a final meeting?

I don't deserve this. The problem with Episcopalians, Helen included, is that they stalk you with silent contempt. So I have a lustful eye, a wayward hand. Is that such a dreadful sin in the grander scheme of things? I believe in salvation. I lead the flock. You'd think that would be enough. I've never understood these people who come to services twice a year, Christmas and Easter, the women decked out in their mink stoles and the men in Wall Street pinstripes, expecting the priest to be an icon of Christian mercy and charity. One hint of transgression and they flash you that sullen look, the Lot's wife look. The pantomime of condemnation. Of course they'll never damn you outright. Out loud, to your face. That would be *un-Christian*. It's as though they've traded in scarlet letters for scarlet stares. And still you're abandoned to the slow, public death of a Puritan under a pressing board. They, of course, are beyond reproach. Even if they make love to their same-sex partners in their spouses' living rooms.

"Please, Helen," I beg, "Can't we let bygones be bygones. There's nothing I can do about it now. Nothing. Helen? Helen? Greta?"

Even if Helen can hear me—and I don't know whether she's deaf or simply obstinate—I know there's no way I can reason with her. She's truly enjoying herself. Her eyes glow, her jewelry glistens. She traipses across the foyer in a drunken waltz and slumps down against the far wall. Her feet tap to the music. The chandelier dances dangerously to the tune of "Chattanooga Choo-Choo," its shadow a flickering ring above Helen's head.

My only choice is to confront Greta alone—out of reach of my wife's wicked spell. Garbo is dazzling, radiant, but shorter than I expected. Her bare legs are almost stubby, like bowling pins.

When she dances, she glides. A stark contrast to Helen's raucous stomping. For fifty years she has been the woman of my dreams, the image in my soul as I caressed Helen's body. Now I have an unhealthy desire to reach out and touch Greta's exposed skin, to tell her that my joke about the sexiest woman on earth was only half a lie. But I am seventy-three: gray at the temples, dead below the waist. What I truly need is a good night's sleep.

"Greta?" I ask. "Can you hear me? If you can hear me, please show me a sign."

She is dancing, pressed to Helen's bosom. She looks over my dead wife's shoulder and stares, mute.

"Can I talk to you for a moment, Greta?" I beg. "Just a minute or two alone? Will you at least hear me out?"

Maybe I have used this line too many times before. She is savvy; she does not trust me. Or maybe she is captivated by the Helen of my youth. In either case, Greta shakes her head and presses her lips into Helen's neck. But timidly. The great Garbo has always sought to avoid public exposure.

I'm crying. The tears singe my cheeks; I make no effort to dry them. I know if I could only have a moment alone with Greta, she'd listen to reason. I'm sure of it.

"Please Greta," I try again. "Talk to me. I know you can talk."

The lovers waltz across the room like teacher and pupil.

"'Gimme a whiskey,'" I say. "'Ginger ale on the side ... and don't be stingy, baby!' Don't you remember Greta? I know you can talk. Speak, dammit, speak."

Gene Krupa answers with a drum roll.

As I gather up the broken china, fear grips me like strong gin. I know what I must do. A quick trip to the *World Almanac* provides the information I seek, a brief phone call offers more detailed directions. The next morning, at half past eight, I drive out to Mount Oreb Cemetery in Greenwich, Connecticut.

. . . . .

The Greta Garbo grave site rests in Block D, Section 128, behind a low hedge of forsythia. A World War II veteran lies to her left; a miniature American flag commemorates his service to God and country. On the vast hills of Mount Oreb, there are other markers as well—flags, cut flowers desiccated with age, small round stones designed to endure forever. In this sea of memorials, the great Garbo has achieved in death what she sought futilely through the last decades of her life: obscurity.

I've purchased a bouquet of white lilies at a small shop across the street, but the austerity of Greta's grave makes me try to conceal it behind my back. I imagine I look as though I'd shown up on her doorstep for a first date. I note the vestiges of past suitors: glass bottles which once contained flowers, the rusted beer can of an overzealous fan. The upkeep is superior at Helen's grave.

"Greta," I say. My mouth is dry, my tongue thick with cat fur. I'm afraid to raise my voice above a whisper. "Can you hear me, Greta? Please show me a sign."

The air is humid and stagnant. Several rows away a young couple stand arm in arm before a marker of rose granite. Otherwise all is silence.

"I know you don't owe me anything, Greta," I say, "I know I'm just a stranger to you. You probably have many strangers come and ask you favors, don't you? So I guess you must be used to it by now. Yes? I'm not sure what I can say to convince you to treat me differently. Maybe there's nothing I can say."

I'm fully conscious that I'm babbling. It's the nature of speaking to the dead, I think. When I went out to Helen's grave last month to make my peace, I found myself conducting a similar one-way conversation.

"Please, Greta," I continue. "All I'm asking is that you leave my wife alone. You know my wife, Helen Christopher. The tall woman with the mousy eyes. The woman you've been dancing with all week. Of course, you know who I'm talking about. I'm not an idiot, Greta, no matter how I sound right now. I'm really a very respectable, upstanding individual. An Episcopal priest in fact. I imagine you're a Lutheran, but the gist of the ideas are the same. The resurrection. Salvation. Turning the other cheek. You are listening to me, Greta, aren't you? Can you hear me down there?"

I'm on my knees again and I'm weeping; I can feel the wet grass staining the knees of my pants.

"Please, Greta, I know what you're thinking. You're thinking that I should take this up with Helen. That I should drive out to the cemetery at St. Paul's and beg her for forgiveness. But she wouldn't listen. I'm sure of it. This is a woman who in forty-seven years of marriage I couldn't convince to re-wallpaper the kitchen. Or have oral sex. But I guess you didn't need to know that, did you? What I'm trying to say is that it would mean a whole lot to me . . ."

I can sense that I'm not making any progress. As a last resort, I clasp my hands and offer a brief prayer. "Please, Jesus, please let her listen. I'm sorry about Helen. I'm sorry about using your time for the other women. I'm sorry about everything, really I am. Please, dear Jesus, please don't forsake me now."

An overwhelming stillness greets my prayers. Even a black squirrel has paused to examine the old man on his knees. I lunge at him with my arms, send him in search of safer amusements. Then I rise bitterly and kick the rusted beer can down the slope. I sense the impotence of my prayers.

"You know she doesn't love you!" I shout. "She's just using you to get even with me. Do you hear me, Greta? Now that she has eternal life, she's showing her true colors. You'll see, dammit, you'll see!"

When I'm done ranting, I toss the lilies onto the veteran's grave and retreat briskly toward the parking lot. The young couple beside the rose marker stares after me. I try to look businesslike and unfazed.

· · · · ·

I pass the remainder of the day watching Garbo and John Barrymore in *Grand Hotel*. The first glimpse of Greta as the ballerina Grusinskaya usually captivates me. Today it feeds my anger. I am alone. I wonder what sort of man lives seventy-three years and has no friend to assist him in his hour of need. Even Dr. Otternschlag's soliloquy recalls my emptiness. "What do you do in the Grand Hotel?" he asks for the millionth time. "Eat. Sleep. Loaf around. Flirt a little. Dance a little. A hundred doors leading to one hall, and no one knows anything about the person next to them. And when you leave, someone occupies your room, lies in your bed, and that's the end."

I shut off the VCR. My own home has become Helen's Grand Hotel and I don't think I'm capable of enduring it another night.

I make my way to the kitchen and search the refrigerator. I realize I haven't had a bite to eat all day. The empty shelves gleam menacingly through a frost veneer. My nightly guests have made off with the food as well as the alcohol. Slamming the door shut, I trudge to the liquor cabinet and pour out the last of the Scotch.

"You beat me, Helen," I toast bitterly. "Are you happy now? You've had your revenge. I confess. I repent. For Christ's sake, Helen, if you have any Christian mercy left in you, you'll leave me alone."

I belt down the Scotch. It burns my throat and boils in my stomach. I've barely recovered when, like an answer to prayer, Garbo's words come back to me. They ricochet through my mind like grapeshot. "But I want to be alone," she says. Her grand statement; her celebrated line. "But I want to be alone."

I stare up into the ceiling plaster, my fist raised in victory. I answer, "But I won't let you, Greta. I won't let you."

. . . . .

Darkness falls and Helen returns to her antics. I can hear her laugher between breaks in the music. Tonight it's Benny Goodman. My body rises and falls with the wild solos of the clarinet. I lie on my belly behind the sofa, waiting for my moment.

The music dies suddenly. Helen and Greta embrace to the sound of the phonograph needle whipping the album label. I watch their farewell kiss. Then I creep from my perch with my weapon in hand.

"Greta!"

She breaks her kiss and looks up at me. Her eyes are cold, indifferent. She is not one to help her fellow man. Yet as she sees me raise my weapon, her blank expression melts into alarm. Her eyes widen. Her jaw drops. Her perfect features turn ugly with fear.

"That's right, Greta," I say as I raise my wife's Polaroid camera to eye level. "I gave you ample warning. I begged. Down on my knees I begged. But you wouldn't even talk to me."

She opens her mouth to speak. I silence her with a wave of my hand.

"Now it's too late, Greta. Now I intend to expose you to the whole world—your most intimate secrets, your relationship with my wife. I'll sell the photos to the papers. To the tabloids. Your privacy in life will come to nothing. In death you will be revealed to the world."

Through the lens, I can see the horror bleach Garbo's face. She suddenly pushes Helen to the floor and blocks her face with her hands. She is too late. The flash blinds me momentarily and when

I look up, the hand is gone. Erased like a pencil drawing. The left sleeve of her dress cuts off at the shoulder.

The one-armed beauty staggers to the door; she fumbles with the knob and then vanishes into the darkness. Helen looks up at me from the floor—her face aflame with indecision. I glare at her menacingly. She turns quickly, follows Greta across the threshold. She is gone forever.

I carefully return the phonograph needle to its perch. Then I wait in the doorway as Helen's Polaroid works its magic. The print is over-exposed.

· · · · ·

My nitwit daughters stop by the next morning. With them is Fred, the son-in-law, dashingly inane in his academic tweeds. He is a rare visitor, his views on religion diametrically opposed to Gloria's. She counts down the minutes to the second coming; he still denies the occurrence of the first. I dread a simultaneous confrontation with the skeptic and the fanatic.

We are seated on the back porch. I pass around a pitcher of lemonade. It is too sour. I add sugar and it is too sweet. I haven't had a decent glass of lemonade since Helen's death.

"So how are you feeling these days, Reverend Christopher?" Fred asks. I can tell he has already answered his own question.

"Ship shape," I say. "In top form."

Anne forks an eyebrow in surprise. Gloria thumbs the pages of *Messianics for Morons*.

"That's good to hear," Fred observes doubtfully. "Mighty good to hear. You gave Anne here quite a scare with that nonsense about Greta Garbo."

I know that I should remain silent, that my problems are solved and it doesn't matter one iota what my son-in-law thinks, that I could sooner convince a slug to swim. But something in his tone—his condescension, his self-satisfied overconfidence—compels me to speak.

"It's not nonsense," I say. "Greta Garbo was in the living room less than twenty four hours ago. I drove her out with Helen's Polaroid."

"Greta Garbo is dead," says Gloria. She nods at the profundity of her observation, then folds her heavy arms across her shapeless chest.

"He's not right in the head," says Anne. She tugs at the padded elbow of her husband's jacket. "It's like I've been telling you all week. He's not right in the head."

My daughters frown with weary, troubled faces: Disguised as concerned strangers, they do not believe me. Fred lights his pipe. He removes his thin-rimmed glasses and replaces them. His appearance reminds me of Joseph Goebbels on the old news reels and I grit my teeth. Don't believe me, Fred, I think. Throw me to the lions, for all I care. I know what I know. Even if I am a minority of one.

"Greta Garbo was in the living room last night," I say to break the silence. "That's the God's honest truth. Your mother danced with her to punish me for my sins. For all of the women—"

"Don't!" shouts Gloria.

But I do.

Anne presses her fingers into her ears as I speak. Fred examines his pipe with feigned intrigue. They are not listening and still I am speaking. Revealing the truth about Greta. And Helen. And me. I know suddenly that I must keep speaking—for my salvation, for their salvation—and that I will keep speaking until they believe me. Until you believe me. I will carry the truth into the streets and I will construct it word upon word like a prophet building a church and I will reveal it in the face of scarlet stares and pantomimes of condemnation and even to the poor fools who frown at me with the ultimate regret of Lot's wife. I know what I know. I will not look back.

Notes

· · · · · · · · · ·

The following materials, derived from other sources, are used as either exercises of "fair use" or are in the public domain, but the original creators deserve credit:

"The Butcher's Music": Rita's remark, "Fresh as if issued to children on a beach," is a quotation from Virginia Woolf's *Mrs. Dalloway* (1925).

"Boundaries": "Do you or do you not believe this man to be Santa Claus?" is a quotation from George Seaton's film, *Miracle on 34th Street* (1947).

"Hearth and Home": Several brief passages from Henrik Ibsen's play, *A Doll's House* (1879) are quoted.

"Silent Theology": "Gimme a whiskey, ginger ale on the side . . . and don't be stingy, baby" is a quotation from Clarence Brown's film, *Anna Christie* (1930); "What do you do in the Grand Hotel . . .? Eat. Sleep. Loaf around. Flirt a little. Dance a little. A hundred doors leading to one hall, and no one knows anything about the person next to them. And when you leave, someone occupies your room, lies in your bed, and that's the end" is a quotation from Edmund Goulding's film, *Grand Hotel* (1932); "But I want to be alone" paraphrases another Greta Garbo line from the same film.

KNIGHT MEMORIAL LIBRARY

DELETE

Jacob M. Appel is a physician, attorney and bioethicist based in New York City. He is the author of more than two hundred published short stories and is a past winner of the *Boston Review* Short Fiction Competition, the William Faulkner-William Wisdom Award for the Short Story, the Dana Award, the Arts & Letters Prize for Fiction, the *North American Review's* Kurt Vonnegut Prize, the *Missouri Review's* Editor's Prize, the *Sycamore Review's* Wabash Prize, the *Briar Cliff Review's* Short Fiction Prize, the H. E. Francis Prize, the New Millennium Writings Fiction Award in four different years, an Elizabeth George Fellowship and a Sherwood Anderson Foundation Writers Grant. His stories have been short-listed for the O. Henry Award, *Best American Short Stories, Best American Nonrequired Reading, Best American Mystery Stories,* and the Pushcart Prize anthology on numerous occasions. His first novel, *The Man Who Wouldn't Stand Up,* won the Dundee International Book Prize in 2012. His second novel, *The Biology of Luck,* was short-listed for the Hoffer Society's Montaigne Medal. Jacob holds graduate degrees from Brown University, Columbia University's College of Physicians and Surgeons, Harvard Law School, New York University's MFA program in fiction and Albany Medical College's Alden March Institute of Bioethics. He taught for many years at Brown University and currently teaches at the Gotham Writers' Workshop and the Mount Sinai School of Medicine.